# WHEN THE EAGLE STRIKES

Ronald E. Gaffney

# WHEN THE EAGLE STRIKES



ISBN    978-1-64552-081-8    (Paperback)
ISBN    978-1-64552-082-5    (Digital)

Lettra Press books may be ordered through booksellers or by contacting:

Lettra Press LLC
18229 E 52nd Ave.
Denver City, CO 80249
1 303 586 1431 | info@lettrapress.com
www.lettrapress.com

# CONTENTS

Ronald Edward Gaffney is a retired lawyer living in Fredericton, New Brunswick, Canada. He attended St. Francis Xavier University in Antigonish, Nova Scotia and later received his law degree at the University of New Brunswick, Fredericton. As a practising lawyer, he had the good fortune to both research and litigate First Nations- related treaty and land claim cases. This legal work increased both his knowledge and interest in the colonial history of Maritime Canada. He is the author of two previous works about this history one entitled "Battleground: Nova Scotia" (December, 2015) and a work of historical fiction entitled "Fire Over Acadia" (March, 2018). He is married with five grandchildren.

# ACKNOWLEDGMENTS

I WISH TO ACKNOWLEDGE the ongoing love, assistance and support of my family during the process of writing this work, most especially my wife Cynthia, my sons Thomas and Charles, and their families, without whom "When The Eagle Strikes" could not have been completed. I wish to provide a special acknowledgment and thanks to my granddaughter Ashley Hughes-Ryan and her husband, Aaron, whose family has a special interest in the history and heritage of Saint John, New Brunswick, an important location in this story.

# GLOSSARY OF TERMS

ACADIANS- The original French emigrants from France to the French colony of Acadia and their descendants. Eventually numbering in the thousands, they created settlements in what are today the Canadian provinces of Nova Scotia, Prince Edward Island and New Brunswick along with portions of eastern Québec and Eastern Maine, U.S.A.

BRITISH- Citizens of the United Kingdom but in the context of this book chiefly those persons from the British Isles, although the settlers in the Thirteen American Colonies were also considered 'British' before the American Revolution (1776-1783).

BRIG- A two-masted, square-rigged sailing ship popular in the 18th century.

CHIGNECTO- An area in southeastern New Brunswick and northern Nova Scotia dominated by low-lying grasslands. Chignecto became the boundary between the British provinces of New Brunswick and Nova Scotia in 1784. It featured an important British fortification: Fort Cumberland.

FRIGATE- Fast, manoeuvrable warship usually featuring cannons placed along a single, continuous deck.

HALIFAX- Founded in 1749 by British emigrants and their military, the town of Halifax on Nova Scotia's southern coast quickly became an important naval base and economic centre.

LOYALISTS- Those American colonists who stayed loyal to the British Crown during the American Revolution.

MACHIAS- A settlement in the southeastern corner of the District of Maine (administered by the colony of Massachusetts) that played a pivotal role in American rebel attempts to capture all or part of the British colony of Nova Scotia during the American Revolution.

MALISEET- A First Nations aboriginal people occupying the St. John River Valley, now in the present day province of New Brunswick, also called 'St. John's Indians'.

MI'KMAQ- A First Nations aboriginal people living throughout much of Maritime Canada and eastern Québec, also called 'Cape Sable Indians'.

NEW BRUNSWICK- British province established in 1784 north of Chignecto, south of Gaspé and east of the St. Croix River.

NEW ENGLANDERS- English inhabitants of the American colonies stretching from Maine to Connecticut in northeastern America.

NOVA SCOTIA- Acquired by conquest in 1713, this British colony, formerly part of French Acadia, was contested by the French and their First Nations allies until 1760. American rebels tried to wrestle control of the colony away from the British during the American Revolution. By the end of the French and Indian War, Nova Scotia included much of present-day New Brunswick and Eastern Québec.

PATRIOTS- Those American colonists who supported the cause of American Independence from Great Britain.

PRIVATEER-An armed private vessel licensed by the government to attack enemy shipping in time of war.

RANGERS- A corps of frontiersmen originally formed in New England and officered by colonists, while the ranks were initially made up of New England First Nations warriors. Later, more non-aboriginal colonists joined the ranks and ranger units were deployed to both Nova Scotia and the northern American frontier, especially New York. Several ranger units were formed by both American rebel and British forces and they mainly fought alongside First Nations tribes on the borders of the Thirteen American Colonies.

SCHOONER- A sailing ship with two or more masts, the foremast being shorter than the mainmast, popular in 18th century New England fishing communities.

SHIP OF THE LINE- The heaviest wooden warships used by the 18th century colonial powers, typically carrying in excess of 70 cannons and 600 men per ship.

SLOOP- A small square-rigged sailing ship with two or three masts.

ST. JOHN'S ISLAND- Now, the present-day province of Prince Edward Island in the Gulf of St. Lawrence.

ST. JOHN HARBOUR- The harbour lying at the mouth of the St. John River in western New Brunswick, home to an important British fortification, Fort Howe, and later the city of Saint John, New Brunswick.

TORIES-Those British and Americans who held conservative, traditional and pro-monarchist political views.

WAMPUM BELT-Indian belt made of shell beads which, when examined by a knowledgeable reader, tells a story or contains a message.

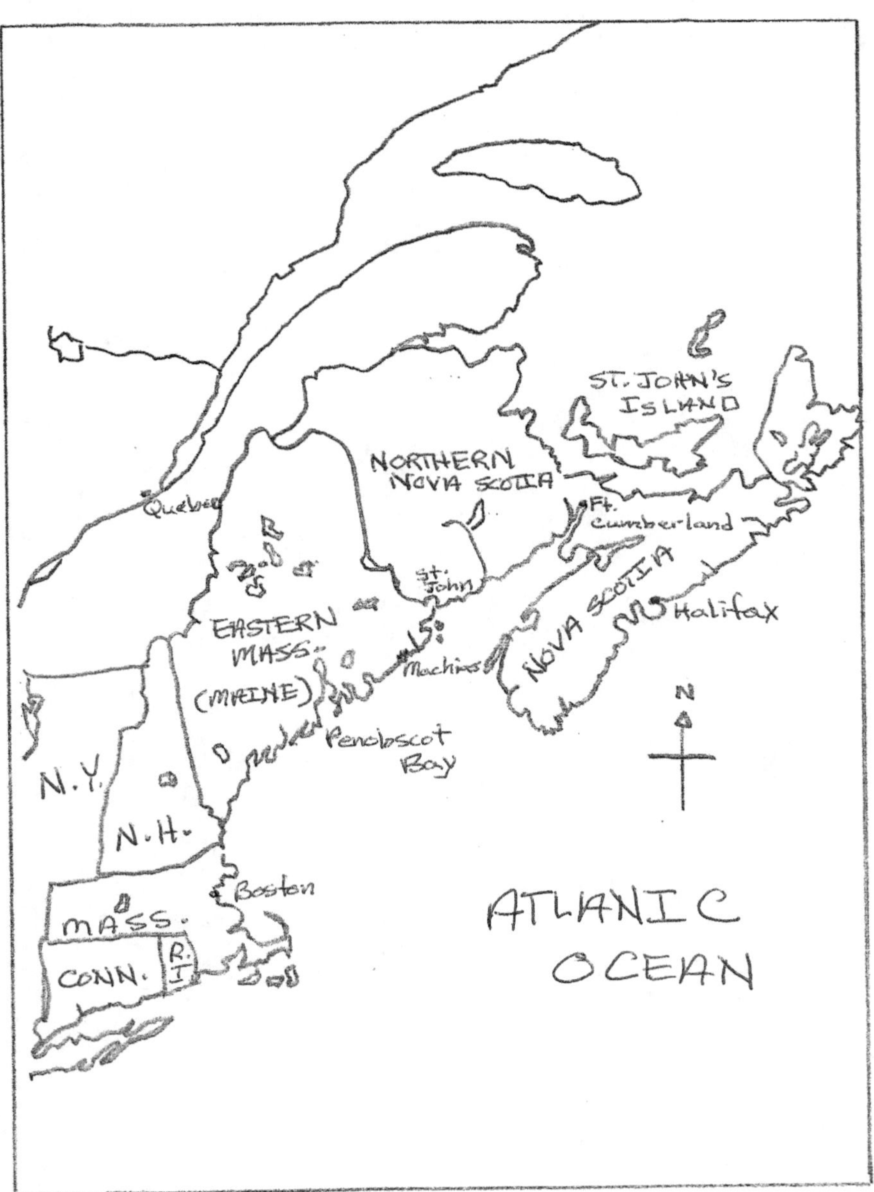

ST. JOHN'S ISLAND
NORTHERN NOVA SCOTIA
Quebec
Ft. Cumberland
St. John
EASTERN MASS. (MAINE)
NOVA SCOTIA
Halifax
Machias
Penobscot Bay
N.Y.
N.H.
N
Boston
MASS.
CONN.
R.I.
ATLANTIC OCEAN

# INTRODUCTION

$F$ROM THE LATE 1760's until the middle of the 1770's a rebellious fever swept over a third of the population of Thirteen British Colonies in America. To a lesser extent, both the neighboring British colonies of Québec and Nova Scotia were touched by this 'fever' but it was along the Atlantic seaboard from Maine to Georgia that the seeds of revolution grew into a thirst for independence and an explosion of violence.

Nova Scotia, once a protectorate of the suddenly rebellious Massachusetts Bay Colony, became an object of revolutionary desire and attempts were made by 'patriot' rebels to invade and plunder the province. Chignecto, perched on the gateway to the peninsula of Nova Scotia, was the centre of much of this revolutionary activity. Frustrated that the large population of New England settlers established at Chignecto and elsewhere in Nova Scotia would not rally to the cause of American Liberty, the rebels unleashed wave after wave of raids, efforts to spark Indian unrest and privateer attacks on the province, driving the loyal population into a state of near constant fear and anxiety. While the Revolutionary War battles fought in and around Nova Scotia were not large, they were sometimes vicious and resulted in great material destruction and economic hardship. American privateer raids were particularly savage and unnerved the coastal settlements of Nova Scotia, especially along the province's south and southwestern shores. The terror did not end until 1783 and the resulting peace lasted less than 30 years.

Our story begins in the early 1770's with our hero, Bryan Hawkins, recounting his life at Chignecto since establishing his "Stonehaven" estate on land awarded him by the British Crown at the close of the French and Indian War. Within a little over a decade after the end of that war, many British Americans were in conflict with the Crown, fighting both British military units and the 'loyalist' armed factions within each of the various American colonies in a bid for full independence. Hawkins, former merchant seamen and colonial ranger, must answer a call to arms once again as the Revolutionary War comes to his very doorstep. With his Acadian wife Gisèle and his four children by his side he must weather yet another storm of violence, this time visited upon him not only by strangers, but by some of his own neighbors.

# STORMS

No SOONER HAD I put aside my ink and quill but emerging events forced me to take them up again and record my recollections. As I indicated in previous journal entries, I, Bryan Hawkins, and my wife Gisèle were settled quite comfortably in our home, 'Stonehaven' at Chignecto, Nova Scotia. We had four children including my first-born, Jonah, two more boys, Mark and Peter and my daughter, our youngest, Heather. We farmed the surrounding marshlands of the Tantramar raising grains, livestock, and vegetables. In the winter months I hunted for animal pelts to sell to visiting traders. By 1773 we were renting modest lots to tenant farmers, mostly New Englanders and then the Yorkshiremen who started arriving in the early 1770's. The New Englanders began to immigrate as soon as they believed that the French and Indian threat had been properly reduced; still their numbers were not enormous as many poor New Englanders now saw an opportunity for free land in the west, given that the French were gone. The Yorkshiremen were recruited from northern England by the Lieutenant-Governor of Nova Scotia, Michael Francklin, to help fill up the vacant Acadian lands north of Chignecto. He advertised an offer of cheap land and a peaceful existence in our province throughout the towns of northern England where land was prohibitively expensive and social change was coming. I came from the south of England and had been in this country since the summer of 1751 when the merchant vessel I was serving aboard was seized by a French privateer. Marooned in Nova Scotia, I came to Chignecto first as a sailor, then as a prisoner of the French and Indians, but later as one of Major Richard Wilmot's company of colonial rangers serving at Fort Cumberland. I received a land grant there as a reduced soldier having served in the French and Indian War.

Fort Cumberland, once an important bastion during the war with France, was abandoned by its British garrison in 1768 as some of those troops were needed to quell disturbances in Boston, the capital of the Massachusetts Bay Colony. As cattle replaced cannons and settlers dismantled some of what remained of the fort's buildings, its ramparts started to fall into disrepair. No one gave it too much thought: France was gone, the Indian Nations were at peace and the settlers at Chignecto were consumed with scratching out a living from the marshes and uplands thereabouts. Many new arrivals found life on the Great Marsh too exhausting and departed. The clever ones enlisted the aid of former French Acadian settlers who had returned to Nova Scotia from their exile by the British in the 1750's.They knew how to work the low-lying diked grasslands. Luckily, I was married to one of those Acadians, Gisèle (Landry) Hawkins who worked with me, side-by-side, to carve out a decent existence on this colonial frontier.

Gisèle and I built 'Stonehaven' together with help from one of our boys (Jonah) and our neighbours, the Dixons and the Whites. Dixon was a former Lieutenant in Danks's Rangers, captured by the French and Indians in a 1757 ambush near Fort Cumberland, marched to imprisonment in Canada and released near the war's end; the Whites were more recent arrivals, farmers from the midlands of England. Our two-storey house was a mix of local brick and stone fitted with two large fireplaces and furniture we built ourselves or purchased from New England. We filled the place with cedar chests, drop-leaf tables, comfortable beds and chairs, rough benches, a fine birch writing desk and a clock, six feet tall, in our entryway. The house sat at the end of an avenue of leafy trees and our stone water-well was situated in our front courtyard. From our rear windows you could see the Tantramar Marsh sweeping out to the Cumberland Basin which joined with Chignecto Bay. We owned a pair of oxen, other livestock, the necessary farm implements and cultivated the surrounding marshlands in the Acadian style. We sold our produce locally and around the province, and shipped some of the excess out of Nova Scotia through the nearby port at Fort Lawrence Landing, just below where old Fort Lawrence once stood.

I mentioned previously the disturbances in Boston which led to the withdrawal of the Fort Cumberland garrison: These disturbances grew in intensity until they spread over all of British North America like an approaching storm. The Thirteen American Colonies, having invested blood and treasure in ousting the French from the continent in 1763, soon found out that Great Britain was not prepared to allow them to reap many of the expected benefits of that victory. Former French and Indian lands in the west which the colonies had hoped would be opened to settlement were suddenly denied to them by the Crown after an Indian revolt prompted Great Britain to close off the frontier by means of the Royal Proclamation of 1763. Parliament then moved to raise revenue to help defer some of the costs of keeping British regiments in America as a result of the Indian war: They imposed a number of small taxes on the colonies, including one by way of the Stamp Act of 1765. Colonial representatives met to denounce these taxes as it was Parliament who imposed them and not the colonial legislatures. As the colonies had no representation in Parliament the colonists saw this taxation as a form of tyranny although, in my view, the taxes were by no means onerous or their imposition an act of tyranny. Great Britain initially backed away from some of its stronger measures, though insisting through legislation that Parliament was still supreme when it came to passing laws affecting the colonies.

Just as calm seemed to settle over the American situation Great Britain decided to impose various 'indirect' taxes on some staple items, including a colonial favourite-tea. Aggravated by prior mob violence, including an incident in 1770 which saw several colonists shot and killed by British troops quelling a riot in Boston, rebellious radicals going by such names as 'The Sons of Liberty' and the like, took to publishing seditious pamphlets and burning a number of British owned ships and custom houses. Actually, the troops in Boston involved in the shootings were protecting the Customs House when a crowd of troublemakers started pelting those soldiers with snow balls, insults and threats. After this disturbance the radicals in the colonies called for even more resistance and began intimidating loyal citizens and royal officials, driving some of them out of their homes and offices entirely. In Boston, a radical mob dumped over 300 chests of tea into the local harbour worth nearly 10,000 pounds as an act of protest against the tea levy and its waiver for an importer favoured by the Crown. King George III and his advisers were not amused: The port of Boston was closed, troops were billeted on the population and many aspects of local town government were suspended in Massachusetts. In February, 1775, the British Government declared Massachusetts to be in a 'State of Rebellion'. The Colony formed a Provincial Congress to manage the new situation and called on its militia to hide arms, ammunition and powder and begin training for a potential clash with British forces. New Englanders began to look upon their own King and Parliament as their enemies.

I learned of these events from various sources including copies of a Halifax newspaper, the 'Gazette', copies of the Boston papers, various broadsides, correspondence that I was shown and, of course, rumours which came ashore with local traders and travellers at Fort Lawrence Landing. The situation caused me great concern and some bewilderment: As New England seethed with rebellion, Nova Scotia remained relatively quiet, especially since the merchant class which now held political sway in Halifax had strong ties to Great Britain. The merchant elite sought to profit from the unrest in New England by seizing some of their trade with the West Indies. Although the colony was filled with New Englanders who sympathized with their kith and kin at home, they, like the Acadians before them, seemed to adopt a 'neutral' stance towards the political whirlwind swirling around them. But not all New Englanders in Nova Scotia were inclined to be passive: One man in particular, a neighbour of mine, Jonathan Eddy, a Massachusetts man, supported all things rebellious. A veteran of the French and Indian War, he had fought at the battle of Fort Beau-se-jour (now Fort Cumberland) in 1755 and for a number of years he was stationed at Fort Cumberland, where we first met, he a soldier and I a ranger; still later he returned from New England to Chignecto as a settler and by 1770 was serving in our provincial House of Assembly in Halifax. Mister Eddy was, in my view, an able and energetic fellow, although a bit of a dreamer. And not all of those who championed so-called 'liberty' were American born: John Allan, a Scot, who came from a wealthy family with ties to the Crown, and who also served in the House of Assembly, fell in with the would be rebels. I personally liked this man as well, if not his treasonous sympathies.

Someone I did not like was a Mister Cedric Coffin, an American firebrand masquerading as an Indian trader. He, too, was from Massachusetts and first appeared at Chignecto as a confidant of Mister Eddy in the fall of 1774. He stopped at 'Stonehaven' one day on horseback, seemingly to purchase food stuffs, but in reality was there to gauge the level of my loyalty to the Crown and the possibility that I might be seduced into joining a treasonous cabal that was forming in the region. Tall and slender, he always dressed in a long black coat with a black tricorn or 'cocked' hat and a pistol in his belt, which he claimed kept him safe in the Indian trade. The man was a snake: You could see it in his eyes and tell it from the way he spoke. I noticed immediately when I met him that he carried very few trade goods with him for supposedly being an Indian trader. He obviously had another employment. Out of courtesy, I invited him into our summer kitchen for a cup of tea. He walked past my family, tipping his hat and smiling. We then sat at my table for some small talk. But the 'talk' immediately turned serious:

He asked me, "What do you think of recent events in the other colonies?"

I replied, "If you mean the plunder and riots that pass for a quest for liberty, I do not think much of them. The radical mobs in Boston would be better off petitioning the Crown for relief than burning royal property and spreading hot tar and goose feathers on innocent bystanders who dare speak up against them. This resort to violence will lead to no good."

His countenance changed immediately and he took on an angry tone and demeanour.

He said, "You call yourself an American, yet you have no sympathy for your brethren now subject to a British blockade, living under the threat of grenadiers' bayonets? Our native blood has been spilled in the streets of Boston by the bloody 'lobsterbacks' (the radical's name for British soldiers). It is time for strong action."

I said, "I do not call myself much of anything other than His Majesty's subject with all the rights of most Englishmen. And what sort of 'action' are you calling for? If you mean taking up arms I am wholly opposed. I served my King during the late war, fought beside both regulars and provincials and took an oath to defend his throne. I have no expectation of tarnishing that oath by speaking treason or acting upon sedition at this late date."

He struck back, "It is no treason to want liberty, self-government, to want to impose your own taxes and defend yourself in the name of freedom without brutal interference from a foreign potentate".

I slammed my fist on the table and roared, "KING GEORGE IS MY NATURAL SOVEREIGN, BY GOD! I was born in Great Britain and have imported my loyalty to this new land. It is unnatural and an abomination for you to contemplate treason and speak of it beneath my roof. What you are advocating is independence from Great Britain and that is sedition. NOW GET OUT!"

He looked at me in a sly fashion while resting his left hand on the butt end of the pistol in his belt. I watched that hand closely. He lifted his right hand while resting his elbow on my table and pointed his crooked finger at my chest saying, "You have a beautiful house. I see that you live quite comfortably. When I arrived here I also saw that you have a very comely wife and four beautiful children. Do not lose it all with misplaced loyalty if your friends and neighbours choose to lift off the yolk of political oppression. Blood may soon be spilled in Nova Scotia in the fight against royal tyranny." He quickly stood up and stormed out. I knew that I would see him again. Those sorts of men do not simply speak their mind, disappear and leave you alone. They are like a recurring nightmare. They always come back.

Gisèle, having overheard our conversation, asked me, "Do we need to fear that man? He seems intent on causing trouble. He is one of those New Englanders clamouring for rebellion."

I replied, "After everything we endured during the late war we have nothing to fear from anyone, let alone that man." This was calculated bluster and she knew it; but I assumed that Coffin was more of a man to watch than to fear. Best be on alert in case he made a move.

Although I detested the messenger (Mister Coffin), the message that the radicals were spreading throughout Chignecto and over much of America was not without some appeal: The promise of personal liberty, being allowed to rise above your station through your own efforts and not by patronage, and being free to chart your own course in life without being told by persons you did not elect exactly what you could or could not do, was a message that found favour with many. But I was suspicious: When I sailed with the crew of my old ship the 'Providence' many years ago, we sometimes visited the southern American colonies, especially the port of Charles Town in the Carolinas. The bad treatment of slaves by some 'masters' at that place made me think that radical calls for universal liberty rang hollow. Few, if any, radicals were proposing that the slaves be freed. Likewise, from early colonial times, the relationship between the colonists of the Thirteen Colonies and the Indian Nations was mostly hostile. Unlike the French, the English colonists made little effort to curry any favour with the tribes, stole their hunting grounds and cheated them in their trade. War followed upon war, mostly over land issues, with the Indian Nations almost universally siding with the French of 'Canada' whenever a conflict erupted. Establishing good relations with the Indian Nations was not a principle espoused by most radicals. Mob rule and violence seemed to me to be the preferred tactics of those who favoured so-called 'liberty' in America. It resembled Anarchy more than Liberty. All in all, I tended to adopt the saying of a renowned loyal citizen as my own philosophy, given the burning populism in the Thirteen Colonies: "Better to live under one tyrant a thousand miles away than a thousand tyrants one mile away."

Despite the fact that trouble seemed far off and most of Nova Scotia was tranquil, there were several disturbing signs: In the fall of 1773, a new Governor, Francis Legge, arrived with a mind to root out corruption in the colony. The 'corrupt' were not very pleased when the Governor's examination of the Public Accounts found gaping holes and missing funds. He set about to rectify past instances of favouritism, fraud, theft and bribery. Unfortunately, the Governor assumed the style and tactics of a street ruffian in going about his investigation. The guilty and innocent alike were caught up in far-reaching inquiries. The backlash against these measures was widespread, but especially among the influential, and there were fears in Great Britain that he would drive Nova Scotia into the rebellious state being experienced in the other Thirteen

American Colonies. And there were several other indications of rebellious sentiment growing in the colony: A tax collector was burned in effigy in Halifax on the slopes of old Fort George in protest of the Stamp Act; a small protest was also mounted near the harbour in support of the action taken against the tea levy in Boston. In addition, the two principal Indian Nations in the province, the Cape Sable Indians or 'Mi'kmaq' and the St. John's Indians or 'Maliseet' were becoming disgruntled. Initially, after the French and Indian War, the two tribes seemed content with the government-run Indian fur trade conducted out of established 'truck houses', or trading posts. In addition, most of their hunting grounds were still intact. But the Lords of Trade responsible for Colonial Affairs struck down the Nova Scotia government's scheme for the Indian trade and opened it up to private traders, many of whom were New Englanders. Complaints were made by the tribes that some private traders cheated and abused them, nor would they extend credit to Indian hunters; in addition, as settlers trickled into Nova Scotia, the two Indian Nations found more and more interlopers within their territories.

In the early 1760's, the St. John's Indians made an armed demonstration and ordered a party of New England surveyors and settlers to retire and settle some thirty miles down the St. John River from the old Acadian settlement at Saint Anne's Point, the party's original destination. The Mi'kmaq, too, cut the salmon nets of Scottish traders trying to reap the rewards of that Indian resource. Both tribes met with the Deputy Agent for Indian Affairs, the former ranger leader Joseph Gorham, laying out their series of complaints. They were promised satisfaction, but received very little of it. In this respect, the situation was starting to resemble the other American colonies. The returning Acadians were also restless, suffering under religious and economic persecution. Forced to reside in the most inhospitable areas of Nova Scotia, they lived a difficult existence. This population might also be ripe for rebellion; but the Catholic Church kept both the Indian tribes and the Acadians in check as best they could at the government's urging. But what if Catholic France were to somehow be drawn into this political turmoil in America?

If trouble were to break out in Nova Scotia the province was in a poor state to deal with it. In 1774 there were less than fifty regulars stationed in Halifax guarding its rotting fortifications. Many of the batteries had been stripped of their cannons, their gun carriages left to decay; palisades and blockhouses had been torn down. The Royal Navy had few ships in Nova Scotian waters, with a handful of provincial sloops and lesser vessels trying to fill the gap. The militia system was a joke. All of the ranger companies had been disbanded. Most of the frontier forts had been robbed of their garrisons and their works were allowed to deteriorate.

Many New Englanders felt that the province was ripe for the picking, especially members of a colony of 'freebooters' established on the Maine frontier at a settlement called 'Machias'. This lumbering and fishing station was hard hit by the closure of the port of Boston and that action fueled a burning rebellious sentiment. Plots to seize Nova Scotia would originate from that place. Meanwhile, the New England militia system was in a state of rebirth, renewal and reorganization. Its members drilled and practised, both openly and in secret, so as to be ready to respond to any conflict with the British Army at a minutes notice. Vast quantities of arms and ammunition were stockpiled in hiding places out of fear that the authorities would seize their muskets and powder, their only means of self- defence. This activity, especially in the Boston area, made the chief British commander, General Gage, and his garrison very nervous, captive as they were on a peninsula next to the harbour. Plans were drawn up to raid surrounding communities where it was thought secret caches of weapons were being stored by the Colonials; also, it was thought several prominent radicals were hiding in these outlying villages. As is usually the case, a war was begun by accident. The British had no intention of tangling with the colonial militia. They had already conducted several small forays into the countryside and had encountered no resistance. They hoped to quickly seize any prisoners and illicit weapons and then hurry back into Boston unopposed, as before; but the militia, now ready to spring into action, were not prepared to surrender their spokesmen or the tools of their mutual defence. They hoped that by simply making a show of resolve, in the form of an appearance, the regulars would conduct an 'about-face' and head back into Boston. Neither side could really conceive of the idea of Englishmen actually fighting Englishmen; yet both sides prepared for a possible fight and then miscalculated.

In April, 1775, forewarned by spies of a British raid targeting the Massachusetts towns of Lexington and Concord west of Boston, the colonial militia showed their resolve and made an appearance. At dawn on April 19th, eighty militia members poured out of a local tavern in Lexington where they had gathered on an alarm raised by nighttime riders spreading the news that the regulars were coming. The militia assembled on their village common. British troops, confronted by armed Colonials, resolved to fight instead of withdraw. In a brief skirmish a handful of militiamen were killed and the regulars suffered one casualty, I believe. The 700-man British force then moved on to the village of Concord and broke into a number of search parties, looking for contraband. One unit confronted assembled militia at a bridge and fighting erupted again. Men were killed on both sides. Militia from the surrounding countryside flocked to the growing violence. The original complement of British troops had to be rescued by reinforcements and together they were harried all the way back to Boston, with the Colonials fighting 'ranger style' from behind trees, fences and buildings. Armed rebellion had been unleashed on the land. There was no going back. The rebellious colonies moved to form a 'shadow' government and a regular Army to be led by a Virginian, George Washington. Full independence from Great Britain became the goal of many.

Wars begun by miscalculation frequently lead opposing generals to believe that the fight will be a short and sharp one ending in total victory for their side. This would not be the case with the American Rebellion: This civil war would burn on for many years much like a raging forest fire rabidly consuming lives and property, pitting neighbour against neighbour, brother against brother, father against son. Women and children, especially those on the frontiers, would also pay a heavy price. Nova Scotians hoped to avoid the approaching flames altogether. Those hopes were quickly dashed. Their brethren from New England, who had once stood with the province to oppose the French and then shed blood at places like St. John River, Village-des-Blanchard and Chignecto would soon return and shed blood once again in some of those same places - but now in an effort to merge Nova Scotia with a newborn republican American Nation.

# DELUGE

T HE FIRST MOVES in the American Rebellion favored the Colonials: Boston was besieged by their militia and a number of colonies combined to finance a strike against the British fort at Ticonderoga, formerly the French fort, Carillon, in upper New York. In May, 1775, that place was surprised and seized without a shot being fired by a force led by a bold American commander, Benedict Arnold, supported by a force of rangers from the Green Mountains. The victors secured an important cache of British munitions, heavy cannons and mortars which they eventually carted off to Boston to aid in the siege. Nova Scotia, too, immediately felt the heavy hand of rebel enterprise when Massachusetts privateers raided my old ranger post at Lunenburg and struck both the Island of St. John's in the Gulf of St. Lawrence and the Canso fishery. While Canso saw its fishing gear and supplies destroyed, various ships torched, and the chief settlement on St. John's Island burned, a Highland regiment raised in America, the 84th, struck back at the Lunenburg raiders: They seized the rebel's vessel while those pirates were still ashore looting the town. The privateers were then rounded up and the first Colonial prisoners were hauled away to be secured in chains on an island near Halifax.

The New Englanders struck closer to home as well. In August of 1775, an armed sloop from Machias descended upon the harbour at the mouth of the St. John River capturing the tiny British garrison holding Fort Frederick and burning the place. They pillaged the small surrounding settlement, roughed up the inhabitants and seized a brig filled with supplies. The citizens of Machias had advocated early and often for American independence. They were among the first to seize a Crown vessel and then to fit out various ships as 'privateers', hoping to prevent British supplies from reaching His Majesty's garrison at Boston. They also sought information from travellers as to the state of British fortifications in Nova Scotia. This rebel enthusiasm, along with the Colonial's stranglehold on Boston, no doubt impressed the New England settlers on the St. John River and the tribe of St. John's Indians, both of whom were now wavering somewhat in their loyalty to the Crown.

Rebel agents such as Eddy and Coffin pressed the Thirteen Colonies to act immediately and seize Nova Scotia; but while the Massachusetts government wrote flattering letters to the St. John's Indians (and received a flattering reply) overall rebel commander George Washington (the same Washington whose actions in 1754 ignited the French and Indian War) did not wish to bite off more than the colonies could chew by launching an attack on a region surrounded by waters that could be dominated by the powerful Royal Navy. Washington sought to bring Nova Scotia into the rebel alliance more by persuasion than force. Still, he was not against supporting a distracting local uprising in Nova Scotia with a few supplies and volunteers, preoccupied as he was at the time with attacking the more dangerous British presence in Boston and at the city of Québec in 'Canada'. Yet, war hysteria was starting to sweep over Nova Scotia: The so-called 'American Party' held open celebrations at Chignecto upon receiving word of the clashes at Lexington and Concord-which made the authorities very nervous. In July, two armed vessels from Halifax were taken by Machias based privateers, who soon swarmed our coast and made the price of goods in Nova Scotia dear. It was rumoured that the rebels had thousands of troops ready to invade the province at a moment's notice and that 'patriot' spies roamed the streets of Halifax. There were several small arsons in the town, including one at the Royal Navy Yard, thought to be rebel actions. The local militia was called out to patrol the town, even at night, but when additional regular troops arrived it was thought best to rely on the garrison to fulfill this function. Trade with the rebels was forbidden and even mildly seditious publications and speeches were banned. Some rural clergymen were even called into Halifax for questioning by the authorities after they had supposedly preached sermons too favourable towards the rebels. Express 'Loyalty Oaths' became popular among those who served in government, the judges and the clergy. Having invited thousands of New Englanders to immigrate and take up strategic lands in Nova Scotia (and who now represented about three-fourths of our population), the authorities wondered if any of their outlying militia units could be trusted. They had good reason to wonder: Many militia captains openly proclaimed that they would not oppose a rebel invasion if it came. Other settlers took offence at being 'forced' to serve in the militia at all, despite the obvious danger to the province. A rumour circulated that militia members would be made to go to England and train for the regular forces. Recent immigrants from the British Isles were desperately sought out to fill the ranks of units that could be relied upon to loyally garrison the province's crumbling forts and sail its depleted collection of vessels designed to guard the coasts.

It seemed odd to me that the St. John's Indians, now leaning somewhat towards the rebels, would ally themselves with Colonials who they had fought so furiously and opposed so often only a decade and a half before: But the New Englanders were renowned traders and the St. John's tribe, like the Mi'kmaq, were now very much dependant on trade for their sustenance. The two tribes had a long history with coastal traders from New England, going back to early French times. The Massachusetts people promised a resumption of the old truck house fur trade if victorious, a measure which found favour with the Maliseet and Mi'kmaq. In addition, the rebels appealed to the Indian's sense of personal liberty. No peoples cherished liberty more than the Indian Nations. Maybe sensing that Americans could be played off against Britons, tribal leaders rarely committed fully to either side at first, waiting to see who would gain the upper hand or make the tribes the best offer in return for their support.

In Boston, British concern that the rebels would fortify the heights near that town with captured artillery caused them to launch a rash assault on entrenched Colonial positions. This mid-June, 1775, attack was led by Major General William Howe-the same William Howe who, as a Lieutenant-Colonel, had freed me from a French prison at Québec in 1759. The British advance was a frontal assault, uphill. With iron discipline and through sheer force of will the regulars drove the rebels from the heights; but in the process the rebels rained shot and shell on the approaching 'redcoats' causing over 1000 casualties. And the attack was all for naught as the British still could not break the rebel's grip on the approaches to Boston. The rebels filtered back into their original positions. The entire area surrounding the city was mostly hostile rebel territory in any case. Despite the receipt of some supplies from Halifax (brought in by convoys designed to repel rebel privateers), their garrison passed a hard winter on short rations within the confines of the Boston peninsula. The commanding British generals – Howe and Clinton (General Gage having been recalled and General Burgoyne having already left for England, bored with the inaction) – decided in March, 1776, to evacuate Boston entirely taking with them nearly 11,000 men, women and children in 120 vessels, all bound for Halifax, Nova Scotia.

On General Howe's arrival in Halifax he immediately demanded lodging for all of his 200 officers and that places be found for his troops and the 1500 'loyalists' who had fled Boston with them. Rents in the town doubled, prices for staples rose and Howe's soldiers began acting as if they owned the place; still their presence was welcomed by a province whose garrisons were undermanned and its population very much on edge. But the British regulars from Boston did not stay long: Led by Howe, they would soon move on in the early summer to other campaigns in New York, Pennsylvania and beyond; but many Boston area citizens loyal to the Crown who had evacuated New England with Howe's fleet stayed on in Nova Scotia and became a new element in the fabric of provincial society. Before Howe left Nova Scotia, however, he made several recommendations to the military establishment as to how to ensure that the province was better prepared to meet any rebel incursions. Not all of his suggestions were implemented: Those concerning the need to immediately secure the frontier forts and the St. John River were largely ignored.

In Chignecto, rebel agitation died away somewhat over the course of the winter of 1775-1776. In preparation for winter, as was our routine each year, the harvest was brought in, the barn was filled with hay for the livestock, preserves were made, meat was smoked and enough firewood was cut to keep the main rooms warm and the cooking fires maintained. Once the snow blew in, forming enormous peaks on the marshlands, we became virtual prisoners on our farm. Snowshoes had to be used to travel any distance. I used them principally for hunting and trapping or to fetch badly needed supplies at neighboring farms or settlements.

One cold December night in 1775, with a blizzard blowing all around our house, Gisèle and I put the children down to sleep, filled the copper warmer with hot stones and placed it within our bed. Just as we were climbing beneath the blankets, I heard a rap on our front door. Gisèle called out for me to respond. Given the unusual timing of the visit and the political climate in Chignecto, I loaded one of my pistols and cautiously went to the door. I opened it to find Gerome, his wife, E'pit, and their three children, two girls and a boy, standing in deep snow, wrapped in blankets and pulling a sled which contained their necessaries, including snowshoes.

Gerome was originally a Mi'kmaq foe who, over time, gradually became my good friend. He had learned more English since the last time I saw him dealing with New England pelt traders at Chignecto in early 1775. He indicated during his current visit that he and his family were on a trek to the east coast and they wished to stay the night on the floor of our house near the hearth. This was not an unusual request, frequently granted to Indian travellers by the Chignecto settlers. Gisèle came downstairs and helped to usher in the family, providing them all with quilts and warming up some soup left over from our meal for them to consume.

After his family was settled, I invited Gerome into my study to smoke a pipe, reminisce about the old days and talk about current events. In the flickering candlelight, with the wind howling and snow pelting my windows, we sat on the floor and traded tales of our encounters in Nova Scotia during the 1750's. Suddenly, in broken English, but utilizing some French, Gerome alarmed me with news that many St. John's Indians and some Mi'kmaq were planning to go and see General Washington in the spring and pledge a number of their warriors, maybe in the hundreds, to the rebel cause. He said, "Our chief men and elders are opposed to this. It is only young men with fire in their eyes who have never seen a fight or taken a scalp or buried the dead who wish it." I asked him how this folly might be stopped and Gerome replied, "Pas d'arrêt. In the Lord's hands now." I was downcast. This news probably meant the advent of a new Indian revolt. In the morning, when the storm had passed, I resupplied Gerome and his family and sent them off on their way to the east coast.

As he left I told him, "I may need to come and see you in the future. Will you see me again to smoke another pipe and talk of war and peace?"

He replied, "Oui, bien sûr." Gerome was still a man of considerable standing and influence within his tribe. I thought it useful to stay in contact with him in case relations between the British and the Indian Nations in Nova Scotia deteriorated sharply. In the early spring I sent off correspondence to the military authorities in Halifax informing them of Gerome's warning. I heard nothing in reply.

In early 1776, General George Washington sent 'wampum belts' among the tribes of the Eastern Indians asking them for warriors to come and join the Rebellion. A number of St. John's Indians and Mi'kmaq answered the call, just as predicted by Gerome. In July of 1776, as the rebels were in the process of proclaiming to the world that they were a new, independent American Nation, tribal warriors showed up at Watertown, Massachusetts to confer with colonial officials. They brought with them a copy of the last treaty made with the British and a promise to sign a new one with the Americans, the first among the Indian Nations on the continent to do so. A new agreement was signed with Massachusetts, very much resembling a trade agreement more than anything else; but a number of those warriors were pledged to the rebel cause and this would eventually have consequences for Nova Scotia. And these Indians were not the only ones to declare for the rebels: In May of that year rebel privateers revisited St. John Harbour and proceeded upriver to terrorize the New England settlers near Grimross and thereabouts. Proclaiming to those settlers that they must throw in their lot with the American 'patriots' or lose their land holdings after a rebel victory, the settlers did just that. And just as Father Le Loutre had done with the Acadians during the French and Indian War, the rebels also intimidated the settlers with a warning that an Indian uprising was coming very soon against the British authorities and in opposition to any settlers who were still loyal to the Crown – the same Maliseet Indians who resided just thirty-five miles upriver at their stronghold of 'Aukpaque' and who had once threatened those New England planters with violence if they did not retire from near Saint Anne's Point.

Despite the rebel victory at Boston and their inroads in Nova Scotia, not everything was going well for the 'patriots': An invasion of Canada in 1775, led in part by Benedict Arnold, had been a total disaster. A rebel force commanded by Richard Montgomery had initial success with the capture of Fort St. Johns below Montréal and then Montréal itself. A strong but ultimately futile effort was made by the rebels to enlist the French inhabitants of Canada to rise up against their British 'conquerors' and become the fourteenth colony in revolt. Catholic clergy played a large role in denouncing the rebels and keeping the French 'habitants' loyal to the British Crown. Meanwhile, Arnold led a second force up the old and exceedingly difficult, Kennebec River route, once favored by raiding Indian war parties during the long series of French Wars. The two exhausted 'patriot' forces finally merged just outside of Québec's walls, facing British forces commanded by General Guy Carleton. Unlike the French commander, the Marquis de Montcalm, in 1759, Carleton let Québec's strong fortifications and artillery do much of his fighting for him. On the last day of December, 1775, a surprise rebel attack on the fortress city conducted in a blinding snowstorm was repulsed. Montgomery was killed, Arnold was wounded and the invading army was left to freeze in the snow. By spring the survivors quickly withdrew to the Thirteen Colonies as a large British Army under the returning General John Burgoyne arrived in Canada. In addition, the Indian Nations of Canada and the west pledged for Great Britain and threatened to set the rebel frontiers ablaze.

Rebel actions were also getting more constructive attention from British authorities in Nova Scotia as well. Besides the 84th Highlanders, made up largely of former Scottish soldiers who had once served His Majesty in various regiments, a number of other new military units were also raised from among the population for service in the province: The Royal Fencible American Regiment, the Royal Nova Scotia Volunteer Regiment, and the like. But, imprudently, no true 'ranger' companies of the type deployed during the French and Indian War were reconstituted, although a number of light infantry companies styled themselves 'rangers'. Loyal settlers in Chignecto kept the government in Halifax fully apprised of the treasonous pronouncements, plans and actions of Allan, Eddy and Coffin, including their petitions and several visits they made to see General Washington and the new rebel Continental Congress, urging them to raise an army against Nova Scotia. Finally, Lieutenant-Governor Michael Francklin of Nova Scotia had enough: He resolved to send troops to the restless Isthmus of Chignecto. In June, 1776, two hundred of the Royal Fencibles were sent up to Chignecto under the command of Lieutenant-Colonel Joseph Gorham, the former ranger leader and Indian Agent. By July, Halifax was offering rewards for the capture of Eddy (200 pounds), Allan (100 pounds) and others. Mister Eddy was in Massachusetts at the time requesting military aid from its government, having received little assistance from Washington or the Congress; Mister Allan, with a price on his head, fled Chignecto for Massachusetts, leaving behind his wife and children. Coffin, who was also sought, boldly stayed on and agitated for the 'American Party'. Many of the formerly 'neutral' New Englanders in the area were starting to hear and respond to the rebel message. The area teetered on the brink of rebellion as rebel privateers imposed a virtual blockade upon Nova Scotia. Communications around a province tied to the sea suffered greatly and even judges and the clergy complained to the authorities that they could not make their required rounds due to the pirates investing our coast.

Gorham hurried to Chignecto and found the remains of Fort Cumberland in a sad state: The ramparts had been worn down by the weather, the buildings partially dismantled by settlers and the curtain wall crumbling. With Gorham's forces having brought few supplies with them in their haste, and getting little cooperation from the majority rebel sympathizers in the area, the 'Fencibles' did what they could to get their barracks and supply buildings in a proper state to withstand the coming winter weather- and any other onslaughts, natural or man-made. Little attention was paid early on to repairing the ramparts; but the Fencibles had artillery, a commanding position on Beau-se-jour ridge, good access to

Chignecto Bay for any resupply and the advantage of occupying the remnants of the old French, and later British, earthworks.

Once Gorham and his men were entrenched at Fort Cumberland he sent word down to me to come up to the fort and meet with him. I took up the invitation, took down my 'Brown Bess' musket from the fireplace mantel (a firearm I had acquired on my return to Nova Scotia from French captivity in 1759), got together my powder horns and ammunition and went to see the Lieutenant-Colonel. I walked the long winding road up to the fort and with the permission of the sentry passed through the gates of a bastion I knew quite well. The fort was buzzing with activity. I recognized Gorham immediately as I had fought beside him at Village-des-Blanchard in 1755. He had been wounded in that fight. I approached him on the parade ground where he was directing the garrison's efforts and introduced myself. He invited me into his reconstructed quarters where he sat behind his desk while I elected to stand. I removed my hat as a salute and show of military deference.

"How are you Hawkins?" he asked, "It has been quite a while since we passed the time at that close-run fight at the French village." I agreed, asked about his recovery from the wounds suffered there, talked about my situation, inquired about his family, then came to the point as to why I had been asked to come and see him. "I need a scout" he said. "The men outside are all very able as a garrison, but I need a ranger-maybe several rangers -to act as my eyes and ears beyond these walls and to carry messages in times of peril. Would you be interested in such a role? I can only pay you a soldier's wages but I had hoped that your past good service to the King would entice you to now serve him once more as one of the few friends I have in these parts."

I was conflicted. I had a farm to run and a family to protect. Should I be caught up in military matters who knew what would happen to both? Yet I was not inclined to have the likes of Mister Cedric Coffin running affairs in Chignecto. I was loyal to the Crown and felt the need to demonstrate it. I had experience with war and knew of its terrible consequences. If I could do anything to head off a war I would certainly do it. And it seemed more likely than ever that a war was coming.

"Let me ponder your request" I said. "I am inclined to take you up on your offer but I must confer with my wife and children. It is upon them that the burden will fall to run our farm and household in my absence."

Gorham said, "I understand. I would do the same. Believe me that except in times of extreme danger I will not interfere with your private responsibilities. Get back to me as soon as you can for I could certainly use your services at the earliest possible moment."

I thanked my former ranger compatriot and left his quarters. I made a quick inspection of the fort and its readiness and found it wanting. While the location had some obvious advantages, I did not know if the British could hold this place in the face of a determined foe armed with artillery and accompanied by Indians. The appearance of the Indians alone might paralyze the garrison and prompt them to surrender the place in a panic.

Little did I know that while I was up visiting at the fort, Mister Coffin and his local rebel outlaws were paying a visit to all of the farms known to be loyal to the Crown, mine included. Coffin and his mob showed up at our doorstep and were greeted by Gisèle. As Coffin had never had an opportunity to speak with Gisèle she pretended that she spoke little English, mostly French. Coffin summoned her out by our water-well in the front courtyard and inquired as to my whereabouts. She feigned an inability to understand his inquiries, talking away in French. He turned to some of his companions and laughed, "I wonder if she could understand my questions if I reached up under her skirt and grabbed her by her 'puffy cake'?" With Coffin's back to her, Gisèle grimaced and grabbed the heavy wooden bucket sitting on the lip of the well, smashing him across his head. Coffin fell forward, almost to the ground, grabbing the back of his head and crying out in pain. He then stood and turned quickly, his face filled with rage, advancing to Gisèle and grabbing her tightly by the throat. He screamed, "YOU FRENCH BITCH, I WILL FLAY YOU ALIVE." Several of his followers rushed to him, grabbing him off Gisèle and admonishing him that this was not the way to win favour for the rebel cause. As he was led away he cried out, "I AM NOT DONE WITH YOU YET. YOU WILL SQUEAL LIKE A SOW AND LAY DOWN BEFORE ME THE NEXT TIME I COME AROUND'. MARK MY WORDS!"

Gisèle informed me of all that had happened when I returned from Fort Cumberland. I comforted her as best I could but, nevertheless, her inner strength and fortitude amazed me. She was quite calm and I knew she was not afraid of that lunatic; but I also knew that I would have to deal with him just as I had dealt with one Alfred Weems, a man who had attacked her many years ago. I later made a search of the countryside for Coffin, but I was told he had left for Machias to assist Mister Eddy. One thing that the incident at the farm taught me was that I could not stand apart from events in Chignecto. I must take up Gorham's offer. I talked it over with Gisèle in front of our children and she agreed. I then went back to Fort Cumberland the next week and told the Lieutenant-Colonel of my decision. He was very pleased and indicated that he would send for me soon, after he had formulated a plan of action.

One night, as we lay in bed, I turned to Gisèle and said, "If the rebels ever return here and I am gone, flee out the back with the children and our valuables – coins, silverware, my pistol case and important papers – and go to the Dixons. The Dixon place is well-protected with shutters and firing loops and Mister Dixon is a former ranger who knows a thing or two about war. He has plenty of muskets and powder in stock. Seek sanctuary there until I come for you. I will gather up the valuables and a woolen sack and I will put them all in a convenient place for you tomorrow. Do not hesitate to go if you see trouble coming."

Gisèle asked, "Do you think it will come to that?"

I replied, "It could very well. There are desperate men coming back to Chignecto to agitate against the Crown. Things could quickly turn violent." In the morning I set out our most precious items along with a pouch of musket and pistol balls and some powder horns which I knew Dixon would find handy in case of trouble. I kept my journal with me.

Unable to convince Massachusetts to send an army to 'liberate' Nova Scotia, Jonathan Eddy, anxious to contribute to the American Rebellion, settled on a plan to first capture Fort Cumberland, with a promise from Boston of adequate supplies for whatever army he could raise out of Machias, St. John River and at Chignecto -but no artillery. Eddy jumped at the chance to command and Coffin, now his henchman at Machias, joined the enterprise; but John Allan, who had recently revisited the Isthmus, recognized the lukewarm support for armed rebellion even among 'patriot' New Englanders living there. He also knew that the Mi'kmaq east of Chignecto, and living north along the coast, were not yet ready to join an open revolt. He carried a mild letter to that effect back to Massachusetts in September after visiting with and failing to sway senior members of that tribe. He and Eddy conferred near Machias and Allan refused to be involved with Eddy's scheme; but Mister Eddy raised almost thirty men at Machias, a handful at Passamaquoddy, and proceeded by schooner to St. John River. Despite past declarations from that quarter in favour of the Rebellion, only a further fifty men – a mix of settlers and St. John's Indians - could be convinced to join Eddy's motley force. Now that the Rebellion was actually upon them, many settlers and warriors showed a reluctance to join in, especially in the absence of a substantial regular rebel army. With less than 100 men secured so far, Eddy's army returned to St. John Harbour and waited for the promised Massachusetts supplies - which arrived late. The invaders were not able to move to the east until the end of October, 1776. Around the same time, Nova Scotia's attention was turned elsewhere, as if by design, when in October of 1776 American privateers laid waste to several south shore provincial towns, including the thriving port and settlement at Liverpool,

Nova Scotia located on the coast west of Lunenburg. Liverpool had been founded by New England 'planters' but this strike had the effect of turning a population that leaned towards the rebels into the King's friends.

A courier from the Fencibles called upon me at my farm asking me to attend at Fort Cumberland and see the Lieutenant-Colonel. I sensed that I would be asked to perform some service, so I got my musket down once again, my old belts and cartridge box from my ranger days, my bayonet, knife, haversack and slung a hatchet in the cradle hanging from my belt. I did not wear my ranger coat or hat, but wore my everyday clothes and a 'cocked' hat instead, so as not to draw attention to myself. In addition, I put together sufficient supplies to carry with me and survive in the countryside for a week or more. I said goodbye to a tearful Gisèle and wailing children, reminding my wife one last time to run from our place if she felt the least bit threatened. When I arrived at the fort I was surprised: The log and earthen defences had been strengthened somewhat and a deep ditch had been dug on the slopes approaching the fort. The garrison was mounting some of the six and nine 'pounders' (cannons) available to them. I went to Gorham's quarters and when I entered I found that he was in a deep discussion with his fellow officers. There was a map spread out on his desk.

"Hawkins, come over here," he said and pointed to the unfurled map. "I want you to see this. We have a report from a loyal settler that there are rebels on the St. John River making plans to head this way. I have sent some of the regiment to establish an outpost at Shepody near the lower Petitcoudiac to give us early warning if any rebel force should come from that direction, but I would like to send you out there just the same to scout and see what you can find. Make contact with our men at Shepody, if practicable, secure the best information and report back to me."

I removed my hat again and examined the map. I indicated my agreement, then left the fort and headed out on the old trails leading north towards the former Acadian settlements that once connected Chignecto with the Petitcoudiac River (now called the 'Petitcodiac' by English settlers). I was basically following the same route that I had come down after being captured by the Indians from the ship 'Salem' back in 1752.

The Shepody outpost was not that far from where Gorham and I had tangled with the French, Acadians and Indians at Village-des-Blanchard in 1755. Little did I know as I headed north that it was already too late for that little outpost: Eddy and his forces landed in boats near the outpost and ambushed a patrol of the Fencibles, killing and capturing a number of them; then the whole of the outpost's garrison was surprised and captured. Having drawn 'first blood' Eddy then went on a recruiting spree, nearly doubling the size of his force with sympathetic settlers and a few vengeful Acadians; but he was largely rebuffed by the Mi'kmaq Nation who wanted nothing to do with a revolt at that place and time, although a few young members of their tribe had already joined with the rebels.

As I approached the valley of the Memerancook River (leading to an old Acadian settlement which I had helped to burn in 1755), an armed gentleman emerged from the bushes and barred my way on the trail. "Halt" he said, "who are you?" I knew from his accent that he was a New Englander and, being armed with a musket and bayonet, he was no hunter but obviously a picket. He was no Fencible, for sure.

I took my chances and declared, "I am a friend of liberty come to join the cause." He relaxed somewhat, letting his guard down and said,"Good thing. I thought maybe..." In the instant that it took for him to relax I grabbed up my hatchet, threw it the distance between us and cleaved his head asunder. The man fell like a stone. I went over to the body and wrenched the hatchet from his skull. It had been a while since I had killed a man. I found it neither distasteful nor especially enjoyable. I felt nothing-certainly not the extreme horror I felt after my first killings back in 1752. I grabbed the bloodied man and pulled him into the brush, hiding my deed. He was no doubt serving as a sentry at the top of a rise overlooking the Memerancook Valley. I crawled on my stomach to the edge of the rise and could see down towards a collection of houses. Among the houses I could see a large body of armed men moving about. Obviously, the rebels were here. I had to get back to Fort Cumberland and sound the alarm.

In late October, the supply ship 'Polly' carrying all of Fort Cumberland's winter supplies, including uniforms, coats, foodstuffs and the like, docked at the mouth of the Au Lac River, slightly northwest of the fort, protected by the British frigate 'Juno'; but the frigate left and the 'Polly' sat captured by the tidal mud flats at low tide. Prudently, a guard from the Fencibles was sent down to the supply ship. Around the first of November I approached the ramparts at Fort Cumberland, identified myself and slipped through the 'sally port' (a small entrance that gave the garrison quick access to the area outside of the fort). I rushed to Gorham's quarters and informed him of what I had learned. He knew with certainty now that Fort Cumberland was the object of the rebel advance. He called out the garrison, doubled the guard and prepared his artillerymen to receive a charge from any invaders-but did not immediately take steps to empty the 'Polly'. I asked to leave the fort to check on Gisèle and the children, but Gorham was afraid to lose any men whatsoever at this critical juncture and requested that I stay on through the immediate danger. I reluctantly agreed.

In early November the rebel force invested the Chignecto area. They raised their flag on a tall pole among a cluster of houses. The banner featured 'stars' and a number of 'stripes' representing the colonies in rebellion. Rebel leaders, including Eddy and Coffin, made their speeches, loudly singing the virtues of liberation and liberty. Mobs started going house to house, at first seizing weapons and supplies from the loyal inhabitants but ominously promising to return. Watching this activity while on a visit to the White household, Gisèle rushed back to our home. She took the children and her bag of valuables, ammunition and horns, and made her way to the Dixon place. Unfortunately, Mister Dixon, the former ranger leader and current member of the militia, had already fortified his house as best he could, left his fearful wife, Abigail, in charge and went up to the fort to provide assistance.

Mister Eddy, meanwhile, could not resist the temptation of the 'Polly' sitting like a lame duck in the mud. On November 7th, using a thick fog as cover, the rebels approached the supply ship, caught the man on guard duty by surprise and threatened his life. He gave them access to the ship and they seized the supplies, the crew and the guards. Unluckier still, the garrison at Fort Cumberland, not knowing that the 'Polly' had been captured, suddenly sent down a work crew to unload the vessel. This detachment, too, was captured. The rebels were able to refloat the 'Polly', sail her to Fort Lawrence Landing and unload her supplies for their own use and benefit. The British prisoners were sent off to Machias.

Between the capture of the Shepody outpost and the taking of the 'Polly', Gorham had now lost a quarter of his men, although some volunteers like myself and Dixon had come in as replacements; but we were a small band of brothers, some too old or ill to fight. Fort Cumberland was short of supplies, its untested palisades were hastily erected and only three of its six cannons were now mounted. Things looked grim. It felt like a rebel deluge was swirling around us. No one at Halifax, or even beyond Chignecto, knew that we were besieged by these 'patriots'. Could we hold out against such odds? Did the rebels bring cannons with them? And had Gisèle and my children been able to successfully flee? The presence of Mister Dixon in the garrison, who I saw upon my return to the fort, gave me concern; but he later assured me that his house was very secure and if Gisèle had made it there she would be perfectly safe.

If Fort Cumberland were to fall I was afraid none of us would be safe.

# SIEGE

GISÈLE SAW THE black plume of smoke rising over the trees. She knew it was coming from the direction of 'Stonehaven' and she knew who was probably responsible. Abigail Dixon was frantic. She had heard from neighbours that the rebels had started to plunder loyal settlers and in some cases were burning their homes. Other plumes of smoke could be seen rising in the distance. The rebels were clearly running amok and Mistress Dixon was afraid. Gisèle was not. "We can deal with this" Gisèle told Abigail, "just come inside." The two women went into the Dixon house, barred the front door with a heavy timber, shuttered all of the windows and placed a musket, shot and powder close to the loop in each shutter. They were assisted by the Dixon's female Negro slave, Zipporah, who rushed about the house caring for the children of the two families, fetching buckets of water to be used in case the house was set on fire by the rebels, and cutting cloth to be used as bandages should anyone be shot or otherwise injured.

It did not take long for evil to rear its ugly head in the form of Mister Cedric Coffin. This time he came alone and not with a throng of rebels. He rode up on his white horse, turned sideways near the door to the Dixon house and called out, "COME OUT HERE HAWKINS, YOU TORY SLUT. I HAVE A NICE PRESENT FOR YOU."

Abigail Dixon cried out softly, "What are we to do? We are not yet ready to repel an assault. We are all going to die." Gisèle said, "Do not worry. I know what I have to do." She turned and went into the back rooms of the Dixon house.

Coffin screamed out again, "I KNOW YOU ARE IN THERE HAWKINS. COME OUT AND I WILL SPARE THE OTHERS. IF NOT, YOU WILL ALL DIE. I WILL NOT WAIT LONG. DO NOT FORCE ME TO COME IN AND MAKE THE INNOCENTS AMONG YOU SUFFER."

Gisèle reappeared and Abigail asked her, "What were you doing back there?" Gisèle replied, "Getting my affairs in order. Stay here. You will be safe." Gisèle removed the timber barrier from the front door, unlatched it and started to go outside. "NO, DO NOT GO. HE MEANS TO KILL YOU AND US, REGARDLESS," Zipporah cried out. Gisèle went nonetheless.

"There you are," Coffin laughed, "I knew that you were in there. I see that your brave husband ran away and left you to me. You should have been at home to enjoy the fine bonfire that I and my fellow patriots set at your place. Your home is now a cinder but I have not yet got what I deserve from you. You and I are not NEARLY done."

Gisèle folded her hands piously and looked down at the earth saying, "I know what you deserve and what I have coming, but not here. Not in front of the others. Go around to the rear of the house, if you please. Modesty demands it."

Coffin was taken aback. He said, "You are a much more sensible girl than I gave you credit." He climbed down from his horse and followed Gisèle to the Dixon's back garden. Once they were well behind the house, Gisèle stood apart from Coffin who looked down, carefully placed his pistol and hat on the ground beside him, dropped his breeches and looked back up at Gisèle saying, "Now where should we begin?" As he looked up he was staring directly down the barrel of one of my pistols which Gisèle had drawn from a pocket in her skirt and had brought to the 'full cock' position.

"We should begin" she said, "with what you deserve and what I have coming." The hammer fell and the pistol roared. The ball passed straight through his head. He flopped on his back, dead. Zipporah came running out of the back of the house, worried as to what had just occurred. "Help me dispose of some vermin I just killed," Gisèle said. The two women hauled the body to the creek that passed behind the Dixon house. Coffin was wrapped in his long black coat. His breeches were down around his ankles. With Zipporah lifting his arms and Gisèle lifting his legs they tossed Coffin's body into the fast running water, pregnant with heavy November rains. It carried him away. Next they threw Coffin's hat and pistol into the creek.

Zipporah said "I will run off his horse. We do not want it found here." Gisèle went back into the Dixon house and told Abigail, "Now we must fully prepare in case more rebels come to plunder this place. Let us collect together all of the remaining muskets, powder and shot on your farm and place them within easy reach. We must bar the rear entrance as well."

Abigail asked frantically, "What happened at the back of the house?"

Gisèle replied, "That mad man fired into the air in an attempt to scare me but then, hearing musket fire in the distance, he ran off in the direction of the fort. The battle there must have begun."

When Zipporah returned Gisèle asked her to maintain the story that she had told Abigail, as Mistress Dixon was a very nervous person. Zipporah heartily agreed. Upon Coffin's arrival at the Dixon house, Gisèle had gone to a back bedroom, took a pistol from my pistol case and loaded it (as I had shown her how to do many times in the past) with a ball and powder that she had brought with her from 'Stonehaven'. She knew Coffin would be stupid and reckless given his intentions and her gender. He was both of those things. He died as a result and ended up in the creek.

With rebels still in the vicinity, Gisèle enlisted Abigail and Zipporah to gather up both families' valuables and bury them in the back garden, leaving out only a few coins and trinkets that Mistress Dixon could spare. Then they completed their defensive preparations, placed some muskets so that they were sticking out of the loops and waited for a visit from the rebels. It did not take long. A group of rebel soldiers arrived at the house, some carrying torches. Gisèle told Abigail and Zipporah to load one musket apiece and for Zipporah to stand ready to reload any muskets that were fired in quick succession. "My boys know how to use muskets as well and will gladly help to guard the back of the house." Gisèle said. She then loaded two pistols and went to the front door once again, turning to say to the other women, "Close and barricade the door behind me. Have the boys bar the rear door and take up positions with their muskets." She went outside and stood holding the loaded pistols across her chest as a rebel soldier approached. This was new to him, being confronted by a woman. He was not sure what to do. He looked back at his men but got no direction from them.

He walked closer to Gisèle and asked, "What valuables do you have to contribute to the forces of your liberation?"

Gisèle said, "Very few, but if you pass us by we will toss you out what we do have. If you do not pass us by those muskets that you see sticking from the loops, and many more being held by others who have fled here, will take down as many of your 'liberators' who are bent on plunder as possible."

The soldier took off his hat, scratched his head and said, "We cannot stay here in any case. We have business to attend to at the fort. Give us what you have and we will be on our way."

Gisèle called out to Zipporah to open a shutter and toss out the small bag of valuables donated by Abigail Dixon. "There is your contribution from us. Now we have been taxed without being represented, so leave" Gisèle said. Gisèle made way for the soldier to pick up the bag. He shook it, turned to walk away, then looked back at the muskets sticking out of the shutters and shrugged. It would appear that there was no sense in confronting such obvious opposition now that the attack on Fort Cumberland had commenced.

"One more thing," he said "Have you seen Colonel Coffin from our Army? We found his horse wandering about just down the road from here. He is needed to command the right wing of our volunteers."

Gisèle replied, "The only 'kernels' I have seen of late are on the corn in the pigs trough." The soldier laughed and walked away to rejoin his men. He did not seem too anxious to find his Colonel. No further search was made. Soon the rebels had disappeared down the road. The danger at the Dixon house was over.

The danger at Fort Cumberland was just beginning. The place was under siege. I had not heard the Indian war cry for a decade and a half; now it echoed across the Great Marsh, giving me chills. Rebels and Indians popped their heads up periodically from behind embankments to fire off a few shots which were mostly well out of range. By November 10th they had encircled the fort to such a degree that no messenger could get through to inform Halifax of our plight. The rebels established their headquarters near the same location that Lieutenant-Colonel Monckton had set up his headquarters during the siege of Fort Beau-se-jour in 1755. Jonathan Eddy sent a flowery note to Gorham demanding that he surrender Fort Cumberland. Gorham not only refused this demand but demanded in writing that Eddy and his compatriots surrender and throw themselves on the mercy of the Crown. This back and forth led to nothing of substance. Now and then, both sides would take casualties-dead and wounded. On one occasion, a Maliseet warrior crept close to the ramparts and shot the man standing next to me near the palisades. As I looked to see where this St. John's Indian was hiding he shot the hat entirely off my head. I returned fire and saw him scampering away towards the marsh. As my hat was shot through, I took the hat off the dead Fencible beside me and wore it thereafter. Poor bastard, I thought.

Joseph Gorham had artillery. Eddy had none. Eddy had to find a way to come to blows with the garrison in the fort without sacrificing all of his men in front of belching cannons. He resolved on a strategy proven successful by the Indian leader Pontiack in the west against a number of British forts: He would have one of his best Indian scouts creep up to and over the ramparts, drop down and open the main gate at the fort to allow a host of charging rebels to storm in. This planned attack by stealth was complemented by the rebel's threatening construction of scaling ladders to get them over the ramparts, in full view of the garrison. The garrison was predictably nervous, cold, wet and hungry. They had lost all of their winter coats and supplies with the capture of the 'Polly'; yet they stood resolute on the ramparts wrapped in blankets and rugs from the barracks in the cold November wind and freezing rain. Most wore their everyday civilian clothes, as did the rebels. When our boys finally received all of their new uniforms in 1777, they proved to be a 'loyalist' green with white facings. Pity, as they could have used such clean, dry clothing during the siege.

"Buck up Hawkins," Gorham said as he toured the ramparts in the most miserable of weather "you and I have been through much worse than this. They nearly had us at that French village back in '55. We were nose to nose with the French and Indians at that time."

I replied, "Indeed we were, but we were also young, hardy and foolish then. I remember that the air was so full of musket balls that you could hold your hat up and it would be filled with lead in a matter of minutes. You could then take those musket balls and fire them back at the enemy." He laughed at this foolish tale and said "Yes, that is true." He then offered me a sip of rum from his flask. I took it and it warmed me considerably.

He said, "What do you think of the rebel effort so far?"

I replied, "As long as you can keep those cannons barking and maintain a steady musket fire, there should be nothing to worry about. They seem a bit timid to come in too close for too long."

Gorham had a serious look on his face. "We have enough ordnance for a little while but cannot go without resupply for long. Hopefully someone has gotten word of our plight to the authorities and I trust no one in Halifax is dithering. I still cannot believe it is Massachusetts men out there trying to capture this place. My forefathers would turn in their respective graves at that prospect and the sheer duplicity of it all." Gorham, of course, came from a famous Massachusetts 'ranger' family-probably THE most famous ranger family in colonial history- having served the Crown since early times. The treason exhibited beyond the fort's gates obviously pained him considerably.

The rebel attack was planned for the night of November 12th. Eddy's scheme had evolved into grabbing our garrison's attention by faking a rush at a strong point in the fort with the rebel infantry and Indians, while a lone Maliseet warrior slipped over the walls at a seemingly unguarded location, opening the main gate to a further flood of 'patriot' soldiers. All went according to plan until, by fate, Mister Dixon, patrolling the perimeter for just such an attempt, came upon the Indian and slashed him with a sword. Although wounded, the Maliseet retired back over the walls to the rebel lines. Now the rebel forces resolved to simply carry the fort by storm: They made several attempts, all of which failed, as a result of the curtain of cannon and musket fire coming from the garrison. Gorham's cannons in particular had a powerful effect, striking fear into the attackers. Finally, the rebels gave up the effort and retired without loss-at least according to Mister Eddy's account of the battle.

As the siege was being managed by a 'committee' in typical democratic American war-making fashion, this single failure resulted in Mister Eddy being removed from his command of the enterprise by the committee. Now a new scheme would have to be developed by consensus to take the fort before significant reinforcements arrived from Halifax, Fort Edward or Annapolis. And it was a relative of Mister Dixon who ensured that help would finally come: This younger Dixon, with three other loyal settlers from the Chignecto area, made their way across the countryside when the rebels first appeared and surrounded the fort. They secured a boat and crossed the Minas Basin to reach Fort Edward and inform its commander that Fort Cumberland was under siege. The armed sloop 'Vulture' was eventually secured at Fort Edward and with a party of His Majesty's Corps of Marines and a detachment of the Fencibles aboard, it set sail to relieve Fort Cumberland.

Disabled by indecision it was not until November 22nd that the rebels resolved to take new action in the form of attempting to burn the fort down around the garrison and then rush in when the chaos was at its height. On two successive nights the rebels came in close to the ramparts and, using some type of flaming incendiary, were able to light several buildings near the fort on fire. They hoped against hope that the fort's powder magazine would somehow catch fire and explode. But the flames never became so widespread and the garrison doused the fires quickly, keeping up a strong fusillade against any approaching rebels, forcing them again to mostly keep away. The rebels eventually retired back to their entrenchments and camps. All the 'patriots' could decide upon at this point was to send word for more help and keep a tight hold on the fort until some form of reinforcement and assistance (hopefully artillery) arrived from Machias or Boston. But it was not from Machias or Boston that reinforcements and assistance arrived, and it was not to help the rebels: On November 27th the 'Vulture' sailed into the Cumberland Basin with its complement of troops. The Captain of that vessel got a message through to Gorham that help had come. The rebels had to have known that the armed sloop was in the vicinity but they simply pulled back some of their encircling forces and reinforced their guard.

Lieutenant-Colonel Gorham brought together his officers and decided upon an early morning attack with combined forces from the fort and sloop in order to scatter the rebels. On November 29th the attack was coordinated and launched at dawn. For the first time His Majesty's forces were in the majority. I loaded my 'Brown Bess', fixed a bayonet and made sure that I had my hatchet handy. With a hearty yell our forces joined together and stormed towards the rebel headquarters. The rebels seemed genuinely surprised by the assault and after firing off a few shots broke easily, leaving their morning meals cooking on their fire pits and their tents and supplies in place, hurrying off in the direction of Green Bay. They even left their wounded behind including, much to our surprise, Benoni Danks, the former commander of Danks's Rangers- Alfred Weems's and Mister Dixon's old unit. Our men were in a headlong pursuit of the rebel's main body. We crossed over some of the same ground where I had fought as a ranger at Fort Cumberland during the French and Indian War, including the spot where my ranger commander, Major Wilmot, was killed in an ambush. Occasionally, musket balls were traded with the fleeing rebel infantry.

Whenever I could I took the opportunity to urge caution upon the Marines and Fencibles. The retreating rebels were now on foot in a largely unknown and unforgiving wilderness which would wear them down quickly and considerably. I felt that we could hunt them down methodically, at our leisure. But having secured initial victory, our soldiers had their 'blood up' so- to- speak. The pursuit was reckless until blunted by a rebel ambush. It took place at a small bridge on the route to Green Bay. Our men emerged from a thicket and started racing across the bridge only to be met by a wall of rebel fire. Several of our soldiers were killed and wounded and the advance came to a sudden halt. As the two sides fired upon one another, I grabbed up a small party of irregulars and we quickly made our way across the modest stream below the bridge, up the opposite embankment and flanked the rebels. When the rebels saw us most of them panicked and ran for the rear, but one came at me with a hatchet. I knocked it from his hand with my musket and I ran him through with my bayonet. I put my foot on his chest as he lay dead on the ground and had to pull with considerable force in order to retrieve my bloody tool of war.

Eventually it was decided that pursuit of the rebels by sea might prove more effective, with some of our forces 'leapfrogging' down the coast to try and outmanoeuvre Eddy's men and catch the 'patriots' unawares. The rebels had made a turn to the west and were now quickly retreating towards the Maine frontier. The

Marines and Fencibles continued the pursuit and most of the militia and other irregulars were sent back to Fort Cumberland. I did not even bother going back to the fort. I went directly home to see Gisèle and my children.

The remnants of the rebel force took well into December to make its way back to Machias, tired, cold and much reduced in terms of their numbers. On the way back home they stopped briefly to terrorize, rob and, in a few cases, brutalize some of the loyal settlers at the mouth of the St. John River. Mister Eddy was largely discredited in rebel circles by his failure at Fort Cumberland but now Mister Allan's star was rising. He had opposed Eddy's overly ambitious plan, but would soon propose a new strategy for the rebels to follow in respect of Nova Scotia.

When I arrived back at 'Stonehaven' I was broken-hearted and fearful. The site was deserted. Where the walls remained, they were blackened. The roof had collapsed into the interior. The interior was a mass of burned timbers, grey ash and, here and there, surviving utensils such as iron pots and metal hangers from the hearths. The furniture was wholly burned. The barn was gone. The livestock were gone. I prayed that Gisèle and the children had escaped the destruction and were not forced to witness it. I rushed to the Dixon house where, seeing Gisèle and my children in the front yard, I ran to them and embraced them tightly. We laughed and talked but Gisèle only informed me of her more terrifying encounters with the rebels much later. The Dixons knew of our family's plight and generously offered to keep us for the winter as it was so late in the year. I gave over all of my coins and any valuables that could be taken in trade to the Dixon family to help with our expenses. My rents from any tenants who had survived the rebel deprivations were also temporarily assigned to the Dixon household. In addition, Lieutenant-Colonel Gorham asked me to stay on as a scout for the Fencibles, so I would still have my Army pay. "We will help you to rebuild in the spring. For now, we will all live together as one family," Mister Dixon said.

Of course, there was a reckoning. Many of the rebel sympathizers, mostly New Englanders, were now burned out by the Yorkshiremen and other 'loyalists', including some of our soldiers and Marines. The Allans and the Eddys and the others who had either taken up arms with the rebels, or had shown an inclination to support them, had their homes destroyed and were forced to wander about in the wilderness in the teeth of a cold winter, over the same snow-covered ground wandered by the escaped Acadians years before. Lieutenant-Colonel Gorham, however, sought out only the rebel leaders and declared an amnesty for lesser participants provided they surrendered up their weapons and took a new Oath of Allegiance to the Crown. This action did not sit well with the regular officers, especially the Marines, and eventually got Gorham before a court-martial. He was exonerated, although his career was tainted ever after. For my part, I thought that Gorham had done an admirable job during the siege. While he made some mistakes (especially involving the "Polly'), promoting reconciliation with minor rebel players was not one of them.

Mercy would only extend so far however. Mister Coffin was sought everywhere in the county but could not be found, until spring revealed his lifeless and decomposing body near the shores of a creek, tangled in some brush. It was assumed that he was killed in battle, but the truth was much more sordid. While we would have risked nothing to reveal the true story, we simply let it go. He did not deserve even a whisper. Likewise, there was no mercy for Mister Danks, the former ranger leader and, like Mister Eddy and Mister Allan, a former member of the Nova Scotia House of Assembly. He was thought to have played both sides before the siege, finally casting his lot with the rebels and breaking all of his prior oaths to His Majesty. His Fencible captors allowed his wounds to fester and he was thrown in the hold of a ship bound for Fort Edward. He died as a result and it was said that he was buried no better than a dog.

The loyal subjects at Chignecto were not the only citizens of Nova Scotia to suffer in the fall of 1776. The infamous rebel privateer John Paul Jones attacked the valuable Canso fishery, not once but twice, in September and November of 1776. On the first occasion he burned fifteen vessels, took others as 'prizes', then went ashore at Canso and other small coastal communities causing great destruction. When he returned the next month he repeated his ship burnings and seizures at Canso and raided a storehouse ashore where valuable whale oil was being stored. Then he sailed around Cape Breton Island raiding Spanish River and setting free a number of rebel prisoners-of-war that were being held there and forced to work at digging coal. In time of war, the fishery was of key importance both onshore, as an export, and to feed the Royal Navy. Any blow to that resource was a serious blow indeed.

Mister Eddy's mishaps in Nova Scotia were by no means the only rebel setbacks in 1776: Major-General Howe struck at the city of New York in July of that year, seizing the place after defeating General Washington on Long Island. Washington tried to block Howe's advance on the city but Howe outflanked and outmaneuvered the rebels who suffered over 1000 casualties, almost double those suffered by our forces. The rebels escaped due to their well-prepared positions on Long Island at 'Brooklyn Heights', across from the Island of Manhattan. These positions held up Howe's forces but could not stop them. The city of New York fell to Howe as Washington continued retreating across New Jersey. British forces held the city until the war's end and it became the chief destination for escaping 'loyalists' in the northeast. British forces also pushed into New Jersey, but Washington pushed back with a daring Christmas assault across the Delaware River, striking Trenton on December 26th, 1776, and defeating a Hessian (German) force. Washington was a busy man around that time for on Christmas Eve, 1776, he penned a number of letters, including one to the St. John's Indians, thanking them for their good service to date, singing the praises of the Massachusetts people in their efforts to establish a new truck house trade with the Maliseet and blasting "the Kings Wicked Councellors" for trying to turn

Indian hearts against the rebels. Not long before this happened Washington met with John Allan about the situation in Nova Scotia and what was to be done about it. Allan outlined his new strategy for seizing much of Nova Scotia from the British.

Mister Allan, who had resisted Jonathan Eddy's rash scheme for Chignecto, now moved to sell a new vision for Nova Scotia to rebel military commanders and politicians. It was a much more limited plan in terms of its territorial scope, but still displayed a degree of audacity. The plan was centred on the Indian tribes of Maine and Nova Scotia, the so-called 'Eastern Indians' or the Penobscot, Passamaquoddy, Maliseet and Mi'kmaq Indian Nations. If those tribes (at least the districts north of Chignecto) could be totally won over to the rebel side then the frontiers of a new American Nation could, conceivably, be pushed from Eastern Maine at least as far as the St. John River and maybe, with a little effort, all the way to the Gulf of St. Lawrence. Few rebel troops would need to be involved-a couple of thousand at most. The fortifications and Royal Navy at Halifax need never be assailed. The plan was all about the rebels seizing more territory incrementally in support of an Indian uprising, creating as much havoc as possible in Nova Scotia.

While our family had been dealt a hard blow by the rebels in 1776, we were alive, warm and together as the year's end approached. We celebrated Christmas that season, decorating the Dixon house with spruce boughs, ate a fine smoked ham, sang songs and drank homemade spirits. We went to our respective services of worship, the Dixon family being Church of England and we being Church of Rome. We hoped that any tests of our strength and will were finally at an end. They were not. As the American Rebellion rolled on we continued to live on the verge of an Indian revolt, with an ongoing threat of rebel invasion and with many more privateer raids to come that would bring a great deal of misery to our coast.

# TURMOIL

ON JANUARY 1, 1777, John Allan met with members of the Continental Congress at Baltimore in the Colony of Maryland. After outlining his plan for Nova Scotia he was well received by the Congress and was appointed Superintendent for the Eastern Indians and a Colonel of Infantry. The title was grand but when he asked the Congress for 3000 men, supplies and schooners to turn his plan into reality he was met with hesitation. He received a portion of what he asked for, all to be based at Machias on the Maine frontier, home of that infernal nest of rebel plotters. Allan undertook all of these activities while his wife and children, having been burned out of their home and seized by British troops at Chignecto, were carted off to a hard and humiliating imprisonment at Halifax. But this fact did not deter him; rather it inflamed his revolutionary passions and he took even greater personal and professional risks to bring about the rebel's desired objectives.

As spring approached, Gisèle and I got to work on rebuilding our lives. With some help from our neighbours we built a small cabin from timber on our lot, then as the weather started to turn warm we went about the hard task of pulling down the remaining walls of 'Stonehaven', clearing away the debris and building a new brick and stone house from the ground up on the same site. It would be called 'Stonehaven Reborn'. More and more, however, Gisèle and our boys were left to the difficult rebuilding process alone as I was called upon to scout for the Fencibles. Thankfully, most of this military work was not local but at this juncture took place at St. John River, given that this was the initial focus of Mister Allan's ambitions.

There was no letup in rebel privateer activity along our shores: In March of 1777, Liverpool, on the south coast of Nova Scotia, was struck again along with many other small and virtually defenseless settlements from the Bay of Fundy, round Cape Sable to Lunenburg. Mister Allan, meanwhile, had started moving back and forth between his base at Machias and the Maliseet settlement at Aukpaque, just above Saint Anne's Point, where he tried to firm up the tribe's support for the rebels. But the St. John's Indians were almost equally divided, half for the 'patriots' and half for the Crown. Allan risked his life with this diplomacy for there were many Maliseet who would just as soon drive their hatchets into the rebel; and the British organized several plots to have him assassinated, none of which succeeded. A bodyguard of Indians who favoured the 'patriots' usually surrounded him when he was in Maliseet territory.

Allan knew that the tribe was usually impressed with bold action so he sought to deliver some: He started gathering together the men, boats and supplies he would need for a raid that might add the St. John River to the rebel camp. The British at Halifax learned of these plans but only reacted slowly and timidly, as they had to the crisis at Chignecto: The authorities sent Colonel Arthur Goold to Grimross and the other small upriver settlements to win back the favour of the settlers in that vicinity. He was backed by a detachment of Fencibles under Major Studholme, who waited at the mouth of the river. Knowing that British troops were nearby, a number of former rebels and some 'neutrals' swore a new Oath of Allegiance to George III and feigned an attachment to all things British-until Goold left. They then largely recanted their allegiance to His Majesty under threats from other 'patriot' settlers and Maliseet who favoured the rebels.

At Chignecto, it soon became obvious that Gisèle and I could not engage in rebuilding 'Stonehaven', plant and bring in a crop, care for newly purchased livestock and cut a winter's worth of firewood simply with the help of our children and busy neighbors. We decided to hire a young Acadian farmer named Pierre Arsenault who owned no farm and needed the wages. Our priest had recommended him and said that he came from a good family. He lived several miles away near the old Acadian settlement of 'Tintamere', north of us. He spoke little English but could communicate with Gisèle in French and we could not quarrel with his work ethic. He was very familiar with building and maintaining the 'aboiteau' system of dikes which were the cornerstone of our farming methods. We invested in a horse which we allowed Arsenault to use and travel to and from work in order to save us time and save his feet from blistering. I found him to be a good worker but rather quiet and sullen.

In May, 1777, Colonel Allan received word that Goold and Studholme had retired to Halifax with their troops, leaving the St. John River unprotected and open to rebel incursions once again. He assembled a force of around 100 men and in whale boats and canoes they made their way up the Fundy coast to a point just west of St. John Harbour. He sent some of his men overland who met with Maliseet from up the river and, together, they approached the settlement that sat around the harbour from the rear. Realizing that there were no British forces about, this advance party went into the settlement, destroyed the property of loyal settlers and took hostages. Then the whole of the rebel force descended upon the harbour, greatly frightening the inhabitants. Leaving a force of fifty to sixty men at the mouth of the river, the rest proceeded to Aukpaque to confer with the Maliseet and show them the spoils of bold action. I was familiar with this headquarters of the St. John's Indians for I had been held there as a prisoner of the

Maliseet and the Mi'kmaq on my way to imprisonment at Québec in 1758. Spread out over a river lot and some islands, the place's chief defence was geography, being located well above the closest English settlement, although it had some timber ramparts; but it was not a site fortified to such a degree that it could withstand a regular army with artillery support.

Allan was said to have been met riverside at Aukpaque with a huge war cry from assembled Maliseet warriors, songs and drumming and the firing of numerous musket volleys into the air. While this warm welcome would seem to indicate Maliseet support for the rebels, it did not. They were still a divided Nation: The rebel faction, led by one Ambrose St. Aubin (sometimes called Ambrose 'Bear'), sang Allan's praises on his arrival; but those Maliseet who took their treaty relationship with the Crown more seriously, and were led by headman Pierre Tomah, held back waiting to see what this rebel had come to offer. Well-schooled in the elaborate protocol of the Indian Nations, John Allan exhibited all of the patience required of him, listening to endless speeches, feasting through endless feasts and providing what presents he could from materials taken from the traders and settlers at St. John Harbour.

In June, Lieutenant-Colonel Gorham sent word for me to come up to Fort Cumberland once again. When I arrived, some of the garrison were apparently preparing to move out. Gorham was pacing on the parade ground. He approached me and said, "Hawkins, we need your skills in the bush once again. The rebels are infesting the St. John River and it looks like they mean to stay. They are inciting the St. John's Indians to acts of violence and we must make a show of force to deter both the Indians and the rebels. I am sending some of my men by sloop to meet with forces from Fort Edward and Halifax, who will then combine and proceed to St. John River and give the rebels a nasty surprise. Can you be ready to go in an hour's time?"

I replied, "I anticipated just such a request and I am ready to go now".

"Good" he said, "let us shower them with lead and hang a few of these traitors. I will be damned if I will let these bastards continue to raid our settlers with impunity, robbing and pillaging as they please. It is time for the iron fist."

This was a new Gorham. Always a tough ranger, he must have been stung by complaints that he was too 'soft' when he did not recommend harsh, widespread acts of revenge against the Chignecto rebels who had attacked Fort Cumberland. Now he seemed to be trying to make up for it. I could care less. I would do as I was told, as always. I had never favoured the strong actions taken against the Acadians and Indians during the French and Indian War but I did my duty nonetheless. I planned to act forcefully against the rebels, but not dishonourably, despite their visiting destruction on my property and bringing terror to my family.

When our sloop arrived at Fort Edward to take on more troops, I went ashore to walk about. The fort had changed somewhat since I was last posted there with Wilmot's Rangers. You could tell that many of the defenses were of recent construction. I assumed that, like Fort Cumberland, Fort Edward had been allowed to fall into disrepair at the close of the French and Indian War and had to be revived with the sudden onset of the American Rebellion. The fort was well positioned, however, to block any rebel attempts to approach Halifax quickly from the rear through the Minas Basin. Soldiers of the 84th (Highland) Regiment, the Fencibles and Marines packed their gear on the parade ground at the fort in anticipation of going aboard the ships tasked to take them to the St. John. In Highland fashion, the soldiers of the 84th not only wore their plaids and 'kilts' to just below their knees, but many carried a 'dirk' or thrusting knife, sometimes in a sheath attached to their lower leg. I noted that this could be a very handy weapon in a close-quarters fight and considered wearing something similar myself.

As I sharpened my hatchet waiting to depart, an officer in the Marines, a Lieutenant Teed, approached me and said, "No civilians are to remain in the fort while we ready. You will have to go back into the town, NOW."

I replied, "I am no civilian, Lieutenant. I am ranging for the troops under orders of Lieutenant-Colonel Gorham at Fort Cumberland." I produced my written orders just so that he would be satisfied, but it had the opposite effect.

"I cannot believe that we have damn colonials serving with us out of uniform. Do you know anything of war, sir, of discipline? When the lead starts flying I plan to shoot any man who does not hold the line and do exactly as he is told. You and the other civilians are therefore warned and should act accordingly."

His comments made my blood boil and I had to respond: "If you read those orders carefully, Lieutenant, you will see that I and the other scouts do not take orders from the likes of you. And have you ever actually been in a war, Lieutenant? I have. Have you ever fought bushrangers or Indians in the forests of America? I have. You would be well advised to watch and learn or you will end up seeing your Marines firing at trees and you will be trying to keep order where none exists." His mouth dropped open slightly and he threw the written orders back at me, stomping off across the parade ground. I thought it best to watch him when we were in the heat of a fight.

As we prepared to depart for St. John River a much larger British force in the thousands was preparing to depart Montréal in Canada under the command of General John Burgoyne. His plan was to head south along the Lake Champlain route and then merge with two other British armies, severing New England from the other colonies that were thought to be less rebellious. Burgoyne's forces were accompanied by a significant complement of Indians and this unleashed widespread fear and panic on the northern American frontier. Militia, woodsmen and American rangers flocked to join rebel infantry led by Horatio Gates (who had served in the British Army under Major Charles Lawrence at Chignecto in 1750) and Major-General Benedict Arnold. As the

British forces inched south encumbered by a long supply train they had some initial success, recapturing the fort at Ticonderoga from rebel infantry who mostly disappeared after a brief fight. But this victory was bought too cheaply and gave the British a false sense of superiority: Burgoyne did not know that the army he was supposed to meet advancing along the Mohawk River from the west had been stopped by the rebels and that the army he was supposed to meet advancing north along the Hudson River was not coming at all. Burgoyne would soon become isolated in the wilds of northern New York fighting men who knew that country very well.

The British collected three armed sloops to transport our men, led by Major Studholme, to St. John River. Although this was a considerable force, we were careful to be on the lookout for rebel privateers as they seemed to be everywhere. Boston Harbour was choked with privateering vessels. The larger ships of the Royal Navy and even its armed sloops found it difficult to bring the fast, maneuverable privateers to battle: They darted in and out of the long coastline they infested, striking quickly then disappearing. The thick fog which descended upon our coast and the many small coves in which to hide made the rebels difficult to detect. The Royal Navy won most of the encounters it had with the privateers, but the hardship was not in beating them but in finding them. We encountered no privateers and arrived at a cove west of St. John Harbour called Manawagonish (or 'clam ground' in the Maliseet Indian language) a place with rocky, tree-lined shores, framed by salt marshes. It reminded me of the Louisbourg landing areas. Studholme's detachment would later be joined by Lieutenant-Governor Michael Francklin in more armed vessels and with more soldiers from the 84th (Highland) Regiment. Landing in barges, our troops encountered no resistance initially and pushed forward through mud, bogs and thick brush towards St. John Harbour. I, and other former rangers were in the vanguard, scouting in front of the regulars. Some of those men had served with Danks's Rangers or Gorham's and a number of them had apparently learned little from their service, at least in terms of a prudent temperament on the battlefield. When we came upon rebel infantry the former rangers engaged them and fought well, holding them in place and serving them up to the regulars. But the fight was difficult: The woods seemed thick with rebels, some of whom were entrenched, while others were hiding in the trees. I could make out one nestled on a branch in a large oak and I aimed just above him. The ball dropped, caught him in the chest and pushed him back against the branches until he fell forward like ripe fruit from the heights. He landed with a huge 'thud' on the ground. Lead whistled through the forest. I saw a Highlander catch a ball in the throat and, choking with blood, collapsed. Some of the regulars were becoming nervous. The Marine lieutenant, Teed, tried to form up his troops into lines of infantry but failed miserably. Soon his men were flailing about not knowing which way to turn or where to direct their fire. Finally, other officers rallied Teed's Marines. They fixed bayonets and charged the dug-in 'patriot' positions. Teed, however, held back; there was no 'leading from the front' with him. As he stood there, almost dumbstruck, a rebel musket ball came tearing through the forest, smashing into his skull. He made a fine target in his uncertainty. Now he was dead as a result.

The former rangers jumped into the lead once again and quickly got in among the rebels, slashing with their hatchets. It was a bloody scene, their axes ripping flesh from bone and severing body parts. The rebels broke and fled. That is when I saw something that I had not seen since 1758: Scalping. Men who once served with Danks's Rangers, in particular, got out their scalping knives and not only shaved the locks from dead rebels but threatened to scalp any living 'patriot' who did not provide them with sufficient information about their friends upriver. Surprisingly, our British commanders seemed to have no qualms about this practice, unlike what I witnessed during the campaigns of the French and Indian War. It may be that these prisoners were considered worthless traitors, deserving of the rope, and that scalping was no great torture involving them. In any case, I still disliked the practice of scalping and stayed away from it. The routed rebels from St. John Harbour fled up the St. John River, past 'Aukpaque' and went as far as the old Indian fort at 'Meductic'. There they took an ancient Indian trail west through the wilderness that would ultimately bring them to Machias. This trail once served as the Indian road to send warriors to ravage the New England frontier and to return with English prisoners to French Acadia. Now it was the chief rebel land route.

John Allan made considerable progress winning over the St. John's Indians to the rebel cause during the early summer months of 1777-that is, until word arrived at Aukpaque from fleeing rebels on their way to Meductic that there were armed British sloops on the lower St. John River and sufficient British soldiers to destroy Allan's small rebel force. The Maliseet were now caught in a dilemma: Should they negotiate with the British, fight or flee? They sat in council and considered their options. As the Indian Nation was again experiencing a divide, the faction under Tomah elected to meet with the approaching British, while the faction under St. Aubin elected to accompany the rebels now heading for Machias. In the middle of July, nearly 500 Maliseet men, women and children in 130 canoes left Meductic to head for the rebel's base of operations in Eastern Maine. At the same time, Pierre Tomah and a Maliseet delegation went to meet Michael Francklin who was now aboard one of the approaching armed sloops. The Lieutenant-Governor had recently taken on the title of Superintendent of Indian Affairs for Nova Scotia-Joseph Gorham's old office, now revived. The need for a more permanent Indian Office seemed obvious at that time and Francklin was well-suited to take on this additional role: He had been a prisoner among the Mi'kmaq during the French and Indian War, studied that tribe's language and customs and spoke French. He promised Tomah a new and better relationship between the British and the Maliseet, to be cemented by a future treaty. Pleasantries and presents were exchanged and Francklin sailed away. But the Maliseet were still not wholly convinced of his sincerity or commitment to their long-term welfare.

While these events appeared to solidify British control over western Nova Scotia, appearances can be deceiving: John Allan conducted a second small raid on the settlement at St. John Harbour (just to accent the vulnerability of the place), but he soon retired. A British move to strike the rebel vipers at Machias produced little of substance: Governor Arbuthnot of Nova Scotia ordered the strike in retaliation for Allan's St. John raids and due to fears that the rebels were organizing a second attack on Fort Cumberland; they also saw an opportunity presented by the withdrawal of rebel resources from Maine in order to confront General Burgoyne in upper New York. The mission was entrusted to Sir George Collier, a navy man, who some say wanted the glory of destroying the Machias base unassisted. While plenty of naval assets were committed to the force- frigates, brigs and sloops- no British Army detachments were included, only Marines.

The British may have taken comfort in the fact that Jonathan Eddy of Fort Cumberland fame was in command at Machias; but no comfort should have been taken. Eddy did an admirable job of fortifying the place, erecting strong batteries and earthworks, and making good use of an infantry force smaller than Great Britain's approaching Marine contingent. In addition, not only did the Maliseet warriors who initially followed John Allan to Machias suddenly make an appearance, but they were complemented by Penobscot and Passamaquoddy Indian warriors who had come to Machias to consult with the rebels. These Indian forces took to the battlefield to help confront the approaching British.

The battle commenced in mid-August and the first attempt by the Marines to land was repulsed. A second effort made under cover of fog was more successful; but while a number of buildings were burned and various supplies destroyed, the main rebel fortifications held. The war cry of the Indian warriors proved unnerving to both navy men and Marines alike and some of the

British vessels coming in too close to the rebel works were peppered with shot and withdrew. The British force finally gave up the effort and sailed away, creating only a minor nuisance for rebel coastal communities in the immediate vicinity.

During the French and Indian War, when Great Britain made an effort to exert control over a region, it usually constructed multiple forts and marched its armies up and down through the contested countryside. But during the early years of the American Rebellion, at least in respect of the St. John River, the place went without a secure British presence and troops came and went, usually followed by rebel raiders and privateers. For example, no sooner had Francklin and Studholme left for Halifax or Minas after subduing Allan's men on the river but Allan briefly returned; then in the fall a new privateer from Machias, a Captain Crabtree, arrived to significantly terrorize the St. John Harbour settlement. The rebels carried off more than twenty boatloads of stolen 'booty' after forcing many of the weary settlers to flee their homes into the forest in order to avoid escalating abuse. As flames licked up from burning structures at the harbour, the most prominent citizens and traders who had already lost so much due to rebel incursions now flooded Halifax with written demands that some sort of permanent military establishment be built at St. John. And the Crabtree incursion demonstrated that some rebel raiders were much more zealous for profit and plunder than they were for liberty.

Meanwhile, as autumn approached, General "Gentleman Johnny" Burgoyne was finding himself in a bit of a predicament: A mid-August raid against what he thought was a lightly defended rebel town quickly turned into a debacle where his forces suffered 1000 casualties. The assault cost him most of his Indian support, as warriors deserted in droves from what they took to be an ill-managed campaign. Deciding to advance nonetheless, Burgoyne cut his communications and logistical train with the north and quickly pushed on towards Albany, New York, even though he knew by then that the British force he intended to meet advancing east along the Mohawk River had been stopped. Major-General Howe at the city of New York had also decided to use the bulk of his garrison to move against Philadelphia, the new rebel capital, rather than remain in place and support Burgoyne if need be. General Washington saw his opportunity, gambled, and sent considerable men and material support north against Burgoyne. This move may have cost Washington the city of Philadelphia, as he was soundly outflanked, outmaneuvered and outfought once again by Howe at a place called 'Brandywine Creek'; but Washington's action ultimately sealed Burgoyne's fate.

The rebels dug in near Saratoga, New York and waited. Burgoyne arrived and his forces engaged in close-in skirmishing over broken terrain and rebel obstacles, such as felled trees, which favoured the 'patriot' side and their ranger style tactics. Rebel marksmen singled out British officers and killed a number of them, in a breach of the 'protocols' of war. Burgoyne threw his regiments against the entrenched rebels several times out of desperation as a rebel 'net' started to form around his forces, squeezing them tightly. Major-General Arnold led a number of suicidal attacks against the British and was badly wounded; but his example greatly inspired the 'patriots' in the ranks, if not his fellow officers, who claimed that he had disobeyed his orders. Rebels flocked to the growing battle like hungry wolves that smelled the blood of a wounded animal. They knew that the British were in desperate straits. The British in the city of New York made a half-hearted effort under General Clinton to go to Burgoyne's aid but stopped well short of their objective. The 'patriot' infantry completely encircled Burgoyne. In mid-October, 1777, when he could not break out of the iron ring that the 'patriots' had thrown up around his forces, Burgoyne surrendered.

Burgoyne surrendered almost 7000 men and lost another 1000 in terms of casualties during the final battles around Saratoga. The losses were so significant, and the proof of rebel martial skills against a European army so manifest, that King Louis XVI of

France resolved to throw in his lot with the rebels and seek revenge for France's losses in the French and Indian War. This news excited the Indians of Nova Scotia to no end, especially the Mi'kmaq, who still had a special fondness for all things French. Settlers in northern Nova Scotia quaked in fear that the Mi'kmaq would rise against them, especially if a French fleet should appear offshore.

I did not even have time to return to Chignecto before I was called upon again to serve at St. John River. While at Fort Edward in Minas, some of the Fencibles who had come back from dealing Mister Allan and his rebels a hard blow were called out to proceed back to St. John River and help to construct a fort at its mouth. I was ordered to go scout and 'range' for these troops. I began to realize that Gorham's promise to me that my duties would not interfere with my personal responsibilities was hollow-but I still needed the Army pay nonetheless, given our family's losses during the Eddy incursion. Major Studholme led our forces again and carried with him by sea the pieces of a 'blockhouse' to be erected and four 'six-pounders' to protect the place, in addition to the cannon support supplied by his armed sloop. A limestone ridge above the harbour settlement was selected as the site of this new fort to be called 'Fort Howe' after our victorious Commander-In-Chief in America. It soon featured a 100-man barracks, palisades, obstacles and, eventually, additional buildings and a new battery of cannons and mortars. The sight of this British bastion high above St. John Harbour deterred all further rebel raids on the surrounding settlement, although the sails of American privateering vessels were frequently seen close to the harbour's mouth. And the fort did not stop Mister Allan's frequent visits to Aukpaque and beyond, through the old Indian trail to Meductic. His lobbying efforts among the Indian Nations would eventually pay dividends for the rebels once again.

Winter was almost over when I was finally released to head home. My service at Fort Howe had been relatively uneventful. I found a vessel willing to brave the ice-free but stormy Bay of

Fundy to carry me back to Fort Lawrence Landing. I learned while onboard that Liverpool, Nova Scotia, was struck again by privateers in September, 1777, and I later learned that this poor town suffered the same fate in May of 1778. A clash between a Royal Navy vessel and a French ship near Liverpool left the French ship crippled and her crew captured; but the wreck became a beacon for rebel privateers seeking the goods, especially arms, left aboard the French vessel. To pass the time, on May 1, 1778, the rebels surprised Liverpool and once again, robbed and abused its loyal citizens. Later that same month they attempted a similar visit, but this time were blunted by the local militia who kept them out of the town. The oft-battered south shore towns were beginning to learn the hard lessons of self- defense: They started to build blockhouses and set up complete batteries (as opposed to a few dispersed cannons) to keep the sea-borne marauders at bay. More importantly, these settlements began to fit out their own privateers, transforming themselves from victims into aggressors: They quickly and successfully began to raid rebel commerce and took many 'prizes' and prisoners; but despite British efforts to disperse more troops and ships along the coast, the rebel privateer plague continued unabated. The rebels now focussed on the trade coming from England and captured vessels such as the Halifax-bound 'Lusannah' whose cargo of tea, sugar and hardware was worth some 12,000 pounds. Some rebels were so bold as to set up temporary pirate 'camps' well inland, keeping their ships at anchor in small hidden coves nearby. St. John's Island was stuck again by privateers in 1778 and wanton destruction, including the killing of livestock, was visited on the inhabitants. No sooner did the King's troops arrive from Cape Breton Island to assist the poor inhabitants on St. John's Island, but the rebels turned their attention to pillaging Cape Breton!

Not just at sea, but on land, rebel activity was evident. Some Acadians on Cape Breton Island became so rebellious that the authorities deported them to France-a revisiting of sorts of the expulsion of 1755. Nor were rebel sentiments confined to the frontiers: More than one toast to ultimate rebel success or favorite heroes (such as General Arnold) was raised in the Public Houses of Halifax. Desertions by both provincial and even some regular soldiers to rebel privateers were not unheard of. The British dared not spread their forces in Halifax too thin around the province, however, as rebel sympathizers circulated the rumour that a force of 14,000 Continental soldiers under Benedict Arnold's command stood ready to invade Nova Scotia as soon as the order was issued by General Washington.

When I returned to the 'Stonehaven' site I was impressed with the farm work that had been completed, but the reconstruction of the house was still taking place at a slow pace. Gisèle and the children greeted me warmly, but when we had time to talk, alone, Gisèle made me aware of an unusual situation: One day when Gisèle was working in the fields with Arsenault, he suddenly turned to her and asked her why she was married to a 'Bostonnais'. She replied that it was really none of his business, but that I was from Great Britain, not Boston, and she had married for love if he must know. He then asked her how she could love someone who did such terrible things to their people. She replied that, as her lawful husband in the eyes of the Church, I was now among her 'people', as were the children of our union. Arsenault replied that he knew that I was a ranger – a cutthroat who had burned Acadian homes and scalped and murdered Acadian men, women and children during the War of the Expulsion. Gisèle replied in a firm voice that this 'cutthroat' paid his wages and he better both hold his tongue and mind his manners from now on. He threw down the hoe he was using at the time, spit on the ground and walked away to our makeshift barn.

This outburst puzzled me somewhat as I had never had a problem with Arsenault before, but I elected to let it go upon Gisèle's urging that, while Pierre was sometimes a stupid and thoughtless young man, he was still a good worker and was needed on the farm until I could be there on a more permanent basis. I asked Jonah-now a strapping farm boy of nearly 19 years-to keep an eye on Arsenault nonetheless. But I could tell that Arsenault was keeping an eye on us as well.

Jonah was growing into a fine young man and was a great help to me. He spoke both English and French, acquired from his mother, who also taught him to read and write in both languages. He became an accomplished farmer and his boyhood companions, the White boys, taught him a good deal about their chosen professions, masonry and carpentry. The more Jonah learned the faster 'Stonehaven' rose from the ashes. While he worked on our farm during the daylight hours, and into the darkness most days, he somehow found the time on occasion (mainly Sundays) to walk to and visit with one Anna Chapman who lived three miles away on a neighboring farm. Her family strictly regulated these visits and I heard no complaints. He proved to be a good example to his younger siblings.

Jonah was now around the same age I was at when I first arrived in Nova Scotia. I came to the province as a sailor and became a soldier. I would not want either profession for my eldest son given the dangers, hardships and brutalities involved. I assumed that he would evolve into a farmer but he approached me one day as I repaired our fenced enclosure and asked if I would consider letting him read the law with a lawyer in Halifax, a Mister Thomas Jackman. I was taken aback. My closest encounter with the law was when the late Major Bradford defended me before the Vice-Admiralty Court in Halifax in 1757 on a trumped-up charge. I did not even know any lawyers personally, although I knew there to be at least one in Cobequid (a town now called 'Truro' by the English planters who arrived there in 1761) and at least two more in Annapolis. Why Halifax? He said, "I have been corresponding with Mister Jackman at the urging of Mister Chapman who is related to Mister Jackman by marriage. Mister Chapman says it is a noble profession for a smart lad like me and he encouraged me." Given that Jonah fancied the Chapman girl, it seemed that this family planned to capture Jonah entirely. I said that I would consider it and speak with Gisèle who would have the final say over our first-born. If he received his mother's blessing to go he would have to find additional work in Halifax, as Jonah told me that Jackman could only pay him a small stipend to help defer expenses while Jonah clerked. Jonah had no problem with that aspect and would find the extra income.

Gisèle was not pleased with Jonah's request to move away to learn a new profession. She and the boy had a special bond as he had been born in the Acadian wilderness and spent the first year of his life with his mother in the frightful conditions of that place and time. Still, the last thing she wanted to do was to hold him back, given his possible advancement in terms of his station in life. She agreed to let him go to Halifax provided he could work out all of the necessary arrangements with Mister Jackman prior to his departure; but she also asked that he wait until the harvest was brought in by the fall of the year, 1778. He agreed.

And then there was 'France': The name alone still struck fear into the hearts of British Nova Scotians, mainly because the English thought that the French Crown still had friends and allies among the province's population in the form of the Indian Nations and the Acadians. But it was not that simple: The Indian Nations, both Maliseet and Mi'kmaq, were still divided in their loyalties between the British Crown and the 'patriots'. The Acadians and the Indians had once put their faith in France and suffered, unsupported, as a result. Catholic clerics could tip the balance one way or the other as religion was a stronger pull on the affections of the Indians and the Acadians than politics or culture alone. Those clerics had been tolerated and occasionally supported by Great Britain, but who knew which way they would ultimately 'lean' once France was fully in the war on the rebel side? As 1778 unfolded, loyalties would be tested once again and the problem of 'France' and her connections to Old Acadia would cause turmoil everywhere-including right on my own doorstep.

# APPREHENSION

IN FEBRUARY, 1778, several treaties, including a Treaty of Alliance, were signed between France and the American rebels. When word of the signings was confirmed among the Eastern Indian Nations it had a profound effect, tilting their political sympathies even more towards the rebels. Yet, despite John Allan sending wampum belts and presents among the tribes, it was still not clear that any of them would actually take up the hatchet in favour of the 'patriots'. They would have to be convinced that France would not only support them but was here to stay. But that was a problem: France was not here to stay. While it might provide muskets and goods to the tribes, it was much more interested in recapturing sugar islands in the Caribbean than retaking its former fur trade empire in Acadia and Canada; and its former Indian allies in Canada and the west were almost universally for Great Britain and against the rebels. These Nations would eventually threaten and cajole the Eastern Indians to abandon their rebel alliance. Initially, however, both the Maliseet and the Mi'kmaq were on the verge of going to war against the British over past abuses, the receipt of promises and presents from the rebels and, eventually, vague assurances of support from the French.

During the spring of 1778 Mister Allan played the 'French card' adeptly and pushed the Maliseet to break with the British and return a British flag to Fort Howe that they had been given to fly over their chief settlement at Aukpaque. He also reached out to the Mi'kmaq who held a series of councils at 'Miramichi' to discuss France's entry into the war on the rebel side. Halifax was concerned when reports filtered in that over 200 Mi'kmaq canoes were seen on Miramichi Bay. Responding to rumours of rebel diplomacy with the St. John's Indians, Michael Francklin appointed a local trader, well-known and respected by the Maliseet (a Mister White), to be his resident deputy on the St. John River. After some searching, Francklin also found a French Catholic missionary willing to go and serve among the tribe-a vacancy that the Indian Nation had complained about for many years. Yet despite Francklin's positive moves, as spring turned to summer the Maliseet seemed ready to cut their ties with England: In August of 1778, the British flag was sent back to Fort Howe with a letter from the tribe which amounted to a virtual Declaration of War. It was purportedly drawn up and signed by the "Chiefs, Sachems and Warriors of the River St. John" but there was reason to believe it was drafted by Mister Allan. The letter proclaimed that the rebels were 'right' and that England was 'wrong', that the St. John River belonged to the Maliseet alone and that American virtue was confirmed by France siding with the rebels. It went on to say that the English King must vacate the St. John River and that all of the English must leave the river now or expect dire consequences. Ominously, it ended with the phrase "Adieu forever"; but the letter was no idle boast for the Maliseet immediately began plundering ships and 'loyalist' settlers, seizing prisoners and demanding Crown payments for both people and goods.

News reached Francklin's deputy agent at St. John Harbour that a large war party of Maliseet, Mi'kmaq, Penobscot and Passamaquoddy warriors was on its way south down the St. John River to besiege Fort Howe and burn the surrounding settlements.

The agent, Mister White, proceeded by canoe north to meet the Indian war flotilla. He encountered 90 birch bark canoes in the vanguard filled with armed and painted warriors. The fleet would have represented a colourful display had their intentions not been so threatening: The warriors were adorned in long coats gathered at the hip by sashes in which hatchets, bayonets and the like were carried. Some wore a crown of vertical feathers, while others were dressed in a mix of Indian and European garb, wearing 'cocked' hats, feathers in a band or nothing at all on their heads. All were heavily armed with British and French muskets and one canoe flew a rebel flag while others flew French colours, probably kept from the last war.

Mister White stood in his canoe, and with a few fearful associates sitting in canoes behind him, beckoned the tribes to come ashore and parlay, which they finally agreed to do. He spent several days in a riverside meadow making every effort to convince the Indian Nations that their future lay with Great Britain, which now had a missionary ready to meet their needs, could provide trade goods and presents much more cheaply and reliably than the rebels and would confirm all that was promised by way of a new treaty managed by Mister Francklin. Eventually, after much laboured discussion, the tribal representatives led by Pierre Tomah (formerly a 'loyalist' but now, given the French alliance, a new rebel ally) agreed to engage in treaty talks rather than combat. This singular act of diplomacy kept the situation on the St. John River from spiraling out of control in favour of the rebels. Now it would be up to the skills of Mister Francklin who, through a combination of promises and threats, would have to work to fully stabilize the situation. All of Nova Scotia would be waiting.

The Eastern Indians could probably rely on 500 warriors to carry out any warlike designs on their part. Throughout Nova Scotia the Crown could probably rely on 5000 troops, mostly clustered around Halifax and along the south shore. The concern was not that the Indians would somehow storm Halifax, but rather that they might lay waste to the small outlying settlements, possibly driving the English from the territory north of Chignecto. This would leave a devastated area that the rebels could then exploit. In addition, the British had learned from the French and Indian War that it was not best for regulars to try and tangle with Indian warriors. Regulars usually thrashed about in the countryside, never able to bring the tribes to battle, while the Indians struck at times and places of their own choosing. It was a maddening type of fighting for the British, thus the need for 'ranger' units adept at forest warfare- of which the British in Nova Scotia currently had none. Halifax, however, was further secured when a full brigade arrived from Great Britain and measures were then taken to help greatly fortify the outlying south shore communities, such as Liverpool and Yarmouth, that were falling victim to rebel privateers. Additional batteries and restored fortifications at Halifax also helped to ensure that no French fleet could suddenly appear out of nowhere and raid that harbour: There was already a problem with the rebels seizing our ships right at the very mouth of Halifax Harbour.

In the summer of 1778 Nova Scotia again felt itself under siege. This was not a novel situation for the British, who also found themselves hemmed in among the thirteen rebellious colonies. Now that France was in the war, the British felt overextended in America and the West Indies given the important locations that had to be defended from its European rival, including its Caribbean islands. Philadelphia, seized from the rebels in 1777, was abandoned by the British in an effort to again concentrate power at the city of New York. But the British were forced to retreat overland from Philadelphia to New York given that a French fleet was on the prowl and sufficient transport ships could not be secured for the more than 12,000 British, German and 'loyalist' soldiers and civilians scheduled to depart Philadelphia. With a baggage train twelve miles long the army set out to cover the 100 miles to New York in blistering summer heat. This target was just too tempting for the rebels: General Washington ordered that the

British advance be slowed by the burning of bridges and the setting up of obstacles in the path of the retreating forces; in addition, the British rearguard was to be attacked. The principle fighting commenced near' Monmouth' in New Jersey on June 28, 1778. At first, the rebel effort was ineffective and almost resulted in a route; but Washington personally intervened, rallied his forces and started trading blows with a British general whose last name I knew quite well-Cornwallis (that is, General CHARLES Cornwallis, the nephew of Edward Cornwallis, former Governor of Nova Scotia, with whom I had a serious dispute in 1751).

The British attempted to turn a rebel setback into a victory but ran up against well-selected rebel positions. Many famous regiments were involved in the clash, including the 42nd Highlanders, Coldstream Guards and Hessian troops-much hated by the 'patriots' for their alleged cruelty and the fact that they were viewed by the Colonials as mere mercenaries from a German state. Enfilading cannon fire mostly kept our forces at bay and, when it could not, the rebels retired to even stronger positions and held their ground. The British Army, exhausted from the daytime heat and stubborn rebel resistance, left the field and retired under cover of darkness. They eventually made it into New York's strong fortifications- a French fleet barely missing an opportunity to trap the British between Washington's advancing men and the New Jersey coast. General Clinton (who replaced General Howe as Commander-in-Chief after the British failure at Saratoga) and General Cornwallis expected a follow-up attack on New York itself, but it never came. While the Generals were relieved that their forces had escaped the jaws of a converging French and rebel army and navy, they were not satisfied at all with their overall position in America (especially in the northern colonies) or the status of the War of the American Rebellion itself: A new strategy was in order.

As the situation unraveled on the St. John River, Jonah and I were off scouring the valley of the Petitcoudiac for a horse for Jonah to use during his weekly (and maybe future) travels. We finally found an acceptable chestnut mount at a farm between Au Lac and Memerancook. While we dickered with the owner over the price, Gisèle was back on our farm making bread in our new pantry. Heather was attending to her education in our study, while Mark and Peter had gone fishing. 'Stonehaven Reborn' was now in a liveable condition and we had moved from our log house into the new structure. Pierre Arsenault was permitted to stay in the timber cottage during work days and occasionally overnight. On the day we were away horse-buying, Arsenault came in through the rear entrance of 'Stonehaven' with a load of fresh-cut firewood. He stacked that fuel neatly near the hearth and appeared to be leaving when he suddenly stopped and turned towards Gisèle. He indicated that he had been talking to his uncle, Marcel, and asked the old man if he ever knew of an Anglo ranger named 'Hawkins'. The uncle allegedly told the young farmer that he did indeed: That he, Marcel, was one of two Acadians who, along with a party of Mi'kmaq warriors, had captured Hawkins in September of 1758. While they were initially fooled into believing that this Hawkins was merely a sailor, they later learned once they had sent him off as a captive to Québec that Hawkins was actually one of Danks's Rangers – a bloodthirsty crew of renegades if there ever was one. Pierre Arsenault knew all along that I had served with the rangers, but it was news to him that I ran with Danks's outfit. It was news to me as well as I had always served with Wilmot's company, never under Danks command!

The uncle further indicated to Pierre that on the day before Hawkins was captured, Danks's Rangers had attacked both Acadian and Mi'kmaq encampments-killing, scalping, robbing and burning everyone and everything in sight-engaging in all of the worst aspects of frontier warfare. While a few of the attacking rangers were slain or wounded, for the most part the Acadian militia and Mi'kmaq were routed, scattered and then they and the surviving civilians spent a very hard winter on the run deep within the Acadian forest, living on meager rations. Many did not survive.

The cruelty of it all was immense. Hawkins, he said, must have participated in these deprivations and it was by sheer luck that he escaped justice. The uncle said that he hoped that the ranger's soul would burn in Hell upon his demise.

Gisèle scowled and told Arsenault that he was misinformed: She knew for a fact that her husband never served with Danks's Rangers, that he was not involved in the attacks on the twin encampments (for she was with me) and that Bryan Hawkins never took part in the more personal atrocities visited on the civil population. He was a warrior, a ranger for sure, but he was no 'cutthroat' or rogue. Arsenault gave her a cold stare and said, "Vous êtes un imbécile et un traître à votre peuple," (You are a fool and a traitor to your people), then walked out.

On our return home with our recently purchased horse, Gisèle informed me of Pierre Arsenault's latest outburst. I resolved on the spot to terminate his servitude but Gisèle interceded again and asked that he be forgiven one last time and kept on. Given her past experiences in the wilderness, Gisèle had a soft-spot in her heart for the other exiled Acadians who had suffered alongside her, and their offspring. I was determined nonetheless to set the record straight with Arsenault, but before I could do so a Fencible showed up at my door and asked that I bring my gear and accompany him to Fort Cumberland to see Lieutenant-Colonel Gorham. No timeframe was given for my expected absence, so I got my things together, said my goodbyes and left with the soldier. An extended mission was no doubt in the offing. Jonah, meanwhile, was outraged by Arsenault's insulting words and actions directed at our family. He secretly resolved to confront Arsenault when the time was right and he had no intention to be in the least way gentle or forgiving.

When I arrived at Fort Cumberland I was informed by Lieutenant-Colonel Gorham that a sloop awaited me and a portion of the garrison in order to speed us to Fort Howe in anticipation of the promised treaty with the Indian Nations. Francklin had sent wampum belts among the tribes inviting them to gather near the fort, parlay and, if agreeable, renew their fidelity to His Majesty. And a measure of intimidation was also involved: The treaty would be held under the guns of Fort Howe, with several armed sloops and plenty of British soldiers, including our Fencibles, within easy reach of the participants. It could be a tense series of negotiations.

From what I observed over the years, Indian diplomacy leading up to and including any treaty council was exceedingly elaborate: First, the person seeking the council must commission a wampum belt of sea shells to be fashioned by knowledgeable women, with the belt representing a summons to the council's planned participants (as a hand written summons would not be well received by the tribes); then runners would carry the belt from village to village along with details of the time and place of the gathering; once the belt was returned to the sender and the invitees assembled, pipes would be smoked, a council fire lit and the wampum would be displayed by the sender (in this case, Francklin) who would stand before the council and deliver a flowery speech flattering the attendees and emphasizing the purpose and importance of the treaty council; a strict protocol was then observed in terms of who delivered responding speeches, with silence being observed by the other delegates; days of speechmaking and nights of caucusing would be followed by a general resolution, and if it was favorable to the sender, a vast number of presents would be distributed and festivities would take place in the form of drinking, feasting and the firing of celebratory musket and cannon fire. It was rare for women to speak at a council, but behind the scenes they exercised considerable influence. The language of the council usually invoked images of 'family' relations ('Our Father, King George' or 'Our Brothers, the English'). Interpreters, some Acadian, usually accompanied each tribal and colonial delegation and I was surprised to learn that the principle Maliseet interpreter was a proud young woman around Jonah's age named Thérèse Tomah, no doubt a relation of Maliseet headman Pierre Tomah.

When our sloop sailed into St. John Harbour in mid-September, 1778, many of the Indian delegates had already arrived with their families in tow: Sachems, warriors, women and children milled about in a forest of lodges and wig-wams located at a cove near the place where our forces had tangled with Mister Allan's rebel raiders. As I walked around the encampment I spotted Gerome and his family setting up a lodge. I hailed him, we shook forearms and embraced.

"How are you old friend?" I asked. "I had hoped to find you here."

He replied, "Très bien. And you?"

"Very good" I said, "I am happy to see you and that we will have an opportunity to discuss events since we last saw one another."

He cast a wide grin and said, "Oui. You and I will have that smoke we talked about at our last visit. Bring your 'tmaqan' (pipe). I will tell you some things you may not yet know. There is a lot going on in secret." I told him I looked forward to it and would come by later with some tobacco.

The treaty council was convened on September 24, 1778, and was well attended by both sides: For the English, Superintendent of Indian Affairs Francklin, Major Studholme (now commander at Fort Howe), deputy agent White and the new priest for the Maliseet, a Father Bourg, were all present. For the Indian Nations, Pierre Tomah led the Maliseet delegation which featured its leading chiefs, including one Francois Xavier, and various 'captains'; but many Mi'kmaq districts were also in attendance including, Richibucto, Miramichi, Chignecto and Minas. Francklin opened the gathering with his 'good news'-a priest had been secured to minister to the Maliseet (Bourg), the British wished to settle all differences with the Indian Nations and reopen a mutually beneficial trade. Then came the 'bad news'-the Bishop of Québec had sent a letter to Bourg stating that any Indians who molested loyal settlers or acted for the rebels would be excommunicated by the Catholic

Church. Francklin then outlined the many lies told by Mister Allan and his agents in the process of deceiving the Indian Nations. Embarrassed by this address, and fearful of the Bishop's warning, the Indian delegates resolved to take a new Oath of Allegiance to King George III, inform the British of any new conspiracies by Mister Allan, forgo and renounce rebellion, make restitution for previous plunders and the seizure of prisoners and henceforth to simply,"… follow their hunting and fishing in a peaceable and quiet manner." All this, they said, would be confirmed by wampum. But just as an Indian delegate was giving this response, a young Mi'kmaq warrior jumped to his feet and, in a serious breach of protocol, seemingly railed against the proceedings. The other delegates had horrified looks on their faces. I noticed the young Tomah woman furiously translating the warrior's remarks into the ear of Chief Pierre Tomah, who did not look pleased. Suddenly, one of the Mi'kmaq headmen barked at the warrior, who gave his senior a look of disgust and stormed out of the council. Things then proceeded on as if nothing at all had happened, with the Indians returning to Superintendent Francklin the presents sent to them by General Washington and a copy of the treaty signed with the Massachusetts government in July, 1776. A new treaty was to be prepared and then signed with the British, the throng drank to the health of King George, and presents of a value in excess of 500 pounds were distributed to the Indian Nations.

When an opportunity arose I went to Gerome's lodge, smoked a pipe with him and asked him about the young warrior who had interrupted the council and what concerns that warrior may have expressed.

Gerome indicated, "You will be surprised to learn that the young man is 'Petite Copage', son of the man you killed during our war. He was born in the season the French fort at 'Siknikt' (Chignecto) was captured by your people. He grew up with a hatred of all things English and he spoke against the treaty, calling those in favour of it worse than dogs. He is a dangerous man for he riles the Indians who still hate the English, but he does not speak for the greatest number of us. He should not have interrupted the speaker during the council and he will be shamed for that. And he nearly created a serious dispute with our Maliseet hosts in their own territory."

Having learned these facts I thought it best to try and avoid the young Copage, but I learned soon after from Gerome that this angry warrior had departed for his home near Miramichi on the northeast coast with a small contingent of those Mi'kmaq who favoured his rebellious views. Relieved of the possibility of entering into a confrontation, the next day I joined in with further celebrations as a consequence of the treaty being signed on the British warship 'Albany'. Aboard that vessel visiting delegates from the Indian Nations and British officials again toasted the King's health, executed the treaty prepared on parchment and then each Indian was presented with a full pound of gunpowder for their future hunting. The festivities then moved onshore again and I got enormously drunk on rum and other spirits. In my stupor I took special note of the beautiful Maliseet interpreter, Tomah, and began to lust after her. She was clothed in a European-style dress and her black hair was braided. I staggered over and spoke with her. She was friendly enough but not really interested in an old Englishman like me. She gently rebuffed my clumsy advances. I then felt quite guilty after the fact, knowing that the woman deserving of all of my love and attention, Gisèle, was at home coping with the running of our farm and the slights of our moody Acadian farmworker. I resolved to curtail my drinking and focus on my own duties, responsibilities and relationships.

On September 26th most of the Maliseet departed the council site for home. As each contingent left the place in their canoes they were saluted with cannon salvos from Fort Howe and the British warships. The Mi'kmaq, however, not to be outdone, entered into a new round of speech-making, wampum presentations, songs and dances followed by the same from the remaining Maliseet. More departure ceremonies then took place and I watched it all, tired and sick from the drink. I said goodbye to Gerome and his family as they prepared to depart, wished them well until we saw one another again and gave him a gift of tobacco, which he cherished. Days later it was time for some of the Fencibles to set sail for Fort Cumberland and I would go with them. I learned before our departure that Superintendent Francklin had resolved to build a truck house at the Indian carrying-place around the treacherous falls near St. John Harbour. It would be stocked with every trade item the Indians may want, at prices designed to undercut the rebel Indian trade at Machias and Penobscot Falls. It was a cunning move and after being rushed into service the truck house had the desired effect of intercepting most of the Maliseet and Mi'kmaq trade. The British policy of demonstrating power, undertaking flattering ceremonies, delivering implicit threats and substantial presents had finally proven successful.

Of course, when Mister Allan learned of the recent, enormous British effort to win Indian favour at the Fort Howe treaty council he was furious- even more so when he received correspondence from the Maliseet Nation (but drafted by Francklin) forsaking the rebel cause and warning Allan and his rebels not to come any closer to Maliseet territory than Passamaquoddy! He immediately dispatched a party of Penobscot warriors and rebel raiders to strike the long-suffering 'loyalist' settlers located up the St. John River in an effort to impress the Maliseet, renew and rally that tribe's support; but the raid had no impact whatsoever on Maliseet sentiments. The Indian Nation now seemed to be firmly in the British camp once again. Allan would now have to look to a new strategy entirely.

While I was gone from Chignecto, Jonah and Arsenault went about their daily chores but circled one another like two wildcats ready to engage in combat. Tired of this game, Jonah finally decided to confront Arsenault near the log house that served as the Acadian worker's periodic residence. He spoke to Pierre in

French. He informed him that should he visit any more insults on the Hawkins family the consequences would be much more severe than simply being let go from his service. Arsenault then replied that this was unfortunate as it would be difficult for him to exercise any restraint given that Jonah's father was a murderer and his mother, a whore. Jonah struck him square in the face with such force that Arsenault fell to the ground. He did not rise up in his own defense but simply smiled and rubbed his chin. He told Jonah, "Ce n'est pas fini" (This is not over). Jonah turned and walked away.

Our returning sloop did not visit Fort Edward at Minas, as was sometimes the case. It was a pity, for I missed an opportunity to meet a person of some notoriety: Flora MacDonald. This Jacobite heroine from the Scottish Rising in 1745-1746 famously helped to disguise, hide and spirit away the Young Pretender, Charles Stuart, escaping pursuing British forces after his defeat at Culloden. She later married one Allan MacDonald in the 1750's and the pair immigrated to the Carolinas. When the War of the American Rebellion erupted he joined elements of the loyal 84th Regiment in the Carolinas and rose to the rank of Captain. Unfortunately, those elements were decimated in a battle there and he was made a prisoner of the rebels for nearly two years. Flora successfully hid from pursuing 'patriots' during this time, but the couple lost their considerable property in the south. Upon Allan's exchange for rebel prisoners, he and Flora went first to New York and then on to Fort Edward where Allan had been made commander of the 84th at that place. Flora only stayed a year, leaving for Scotland in the fall of 1779. I am told that she not only remained feisty in Nova Scotia, but on her voyage home she was wounded in a fight between the ship she was travelling aboard and a French privateer after refusing to go below with the other dependants. She eventually made it to Scotland, however, recovered and was joined by her husband at the end of his service in 1784. It has always amazed me how Jacobite Scots could elect to fight for their former Hanoverian opponents (George II and III) who they once so fiercely opposed, not as mercenaries, but out of loyalty to their oath and clan.

I arrived back in Chignecto in the first part of October. The Captain of our sloop decided to anchor near the mouth of the Au Lac River (the same spot where the ship 'Polly' had been captured and taken away by the rebels in 1776) for the convenience of the departing Fencibles. When I returned to Fort Cumberland I found Jonah there, carrying caribou meat for the garrison and hides slung across his horse, for trading. He had shot and skinned two of these large deer and, given that our family was already well-provisioned for the fall and winter, he thought it might be a good gesture to supply those troops with whom I sometimes served with some fresh meat. I yelled to Jonah, embraced him and celebrated our reunion. I told him that I had a report to make to the Lieutenant-Colonel concerning the Fort Howe treaty and suggested that once his business was done at the fort he should ride back to our farm and tell his mother and siblings that I would be home directly. He agreed.

Jonah quickly concluded his affairs at the fort and rushed back to 'Stonehaven Reborn'. When he entered the house he found his mother cooking a wild meat stew hanging over the fire and Pierre Arsenault bringing in bundles of kindling. He gave Arsenault an icy stare then asked his mother, "Where are Mark, Peter and Heather?"

Gisèle explained that they were up the stairs cleaning the place. Jonah then said, "Well, father is home. He is at the fort now, but I expect him soon."

A smile lit up Gisèle's face and she yelled for the other children to come down the stairs. Jonah turned to look for any reaction from Arsenault, but the Acadian was gone. He had dropped the split kindling in a haphazard manner on the floor. Jonah was puzzled and wandered out into the front yard to see what Arsenault was up to. The yard was empty. Jonah walked towards the log house used by Arsenault, then changed his mind, turned around and walked back towards the front of our house. To Hell with him, he thought.

Then he heard the 'crack' of a musket being fired.

The lead ball tore through his right shoulder from the rear, knocking him forward on his face in the process. He lay there in the dirt in incredible pain, unable to move. His right arm was frozen. He could make out a shadow beside him. It was Arsenault. The Acadian made a 'huffing' noise then walked towards the front of the house. Inside, Gisèle heard the shot. She probably assumed that hunters were firing at some game too close to the house, which had happened in the past. She started for the front door but heard the three children on the stairs. Probably feeling uneasy and not knowing what she would find outside our front door she went over to the staircase and ordered them back upstairs. "Do not come down here until I tell you to," she said. She turned and walked back towards the front door. It burst open. There was Pierre Arsenault, armed with his musket, carrying a pistol in his belt and displaying a wild look in his eyes. He rushed in, closed the door behind him and pushed an advancing Gisèle across the room with the musket. "MON DIEU" she screamed. Mark meanwhile had crept to the top of the stairs to witness what was happening.

Once Arsenault had forced Gisèle back across the room, he pushed her into a high-backed 'Clergy Bench' resting along our far wall. He grabbed her by the back of her collar, sat her down, put his musket aside, sat beside her and drew the pistol, cocking it and placing it to her temple. "Maintenant nous attendons," (Now we wait) he said. Gisèle struggled but she was tiny and Arsenault was larger, stronger and appeared focussed.

I arrived at 'Stonehaven' and saw a body lying face-down in my front yard. Not knowing what I was about to confront, I crept from tree to tree in front of our house, then quickly to the stone water-well near our place. There appeared to be no one in any of the windows or concealed nearby, so I ran to the body in the yard in a 'hunched-over' position. It was, of course, Jonah. He looked up slightly over his left shoulder and said, "It is Arsenault. He is inside and he is armed." I moved to the left side of our front door and quickly loaded my musket. Time to settle accounts.

Arsenault may have assumed that, in my fury, I would simply throw open the front door and charge in. Mark watched him alternate between holding the pistol to Gisèle's head and pointing it directly at the far door. He was suddenly nervous, sweating and shaking- full of apprehension. Seconds turned into minutes. All was quiet. I knew that I had to end things. I took up my hatchet, reached over with it and depressed the door latch. I then pushed the door inward with the hatchet, pulling back quickly. Arsenault was a bundle of nerves. Gisèle, knowing that Arsenault was distracted, lurched forward and broke free, running for the opening door. She screamed, "NO BRYAN..." Arsenault panicked, stood and fired. The ball struck Gisèle in the back of the head near the top of her neck. I believe that she died instantly. I appeared in the doorway, hoping that Arsenault had no second pistol. He did not. His eyes were as wide as two full moons and his mouth dropped open. He knew in that instant that he was about to die. And he did. The blast from my musket threw him back into the bench behind him and he slumped forward. I knelt beside Gisèle and cried. We never even had a chance to say goodbye to one another. The three children ran down the stairs. I caught Mark and told him, "Your brother has been shot. Get his horse, ride to the fort, inform Lieutenant-Colonel Gorham and tell him to bring his Surgeon and some troops. Hurry now." Mark promptly followed my instructions.

The Surgeon arrived and saw to it that Jonah was carried into our house by the Fencibles and placed on our largest table, where he worked on him. The Surgeon was able to secure the ball, burn and bandage the wound. The Lieutenant-Colonel surveyed the blood-soaked death scene and I told him my version of events. "You will have to be held at the guardhouse at the fort until this can all be sorted out," Gorham said. I had no objection. I had seen the inside of a guardhouse before. He indicated that he would send a soldier to fetch the Sheriff who was believed to be at the village of "Les Planches" nearby, who would then come and observe, investigate and interview witnesses to these horrific events. I sent Mark off on horseback to secure our Priest to the north in 'Tintamere' as Gisèle would have to be laid to rest. She was wrapped in a shroud for now and, at some point, a funeral Mass would be said for her-though it looked doubtful that I would be able to attend. Gorham allowed me to remain at our house under guard until both the Priest and Sheriff arrived and I could speak with each. There was an air of suspicion and prejudice surrounding the meeting as Catholic and Protestant rarely converged in any official capacities; in fact, Catholic priests were still forbidden by law from performing many official functions. Eventually everything was arranged, however, and I was marched off to the Fort Cumberland guardhouse to await the final results of the investigation.

Gisèle was buried in a Catholic cemetery near Memerancook among her Acadian brethren. Her immediate family were all deceased and the rest scattered by the British expulsions beginning in 1755. My children Mark, Peter and Heather, accompanied by a contingent of Fencibles dispatched by Gorham, attended at the French burial service. I remained confined at Fort Cumberland and Jonah was cared for quite well by Mistress Dixon and Anna Chapman, his good friend and neighbor. I do not know when and where Arsenault was buried and did not care to know at the time. After reviewing the scene of Arsenault's killing, talking with our son, Mark (who had a full view of indoor events) and Jonah (who had a full view of outdoor events) and others, it was finally determined by the Sheriff that no Indictment would be sworn out against me for murder or any other sort of unlawful killing, it being a clear case of self-defence and defence of my family. I was finally released and returned to care for my wounded son and remaining children.

We were alone. 'Stronehaven Reborn' seemed like a hollow shell to me now. I visited Gisèle's grave several times but felt uneasy.

Maybe my life was over as well; yet no sooner did those thoughts intrude but I knew that I had to stay strong and comforting for our children. Still, other dark thoughts also crowded in: What really killed Gisèle? Was it simply the ball from Arsenault's pistol – a cruel twist of fate? Or did she die as God's punishment for my yearnings for the young Tomah girl? Or was it God's vengeance for my past wicked deeds, including the murders of Delahunt and Weems? I was driven mad with guilt and my headaches (first experienced during my early days in Nova Scotia) returned more frequently to bother me. And my sleep was plagued with nightmares of past battles, dead foes and poor Gisèle.

A thirst for vengeance and misinformation had brought my family in Nova Scotia to a cruel crossroads. In the Thirteen American Colonies, a thirst for quick victories and plenty of misunderstandings had led the British military to a crossroads of sorts as well: The military's power had been applied haphazardly, little effort had been devoted to winning back the hearts of the rebellious colonists and British skill had been more than matched by 'patriot' luck and endurance. The British strategy must change: The British eyed the southernmost American colonies. It was thought that there was a larger 'loyalist' population there than in the north who would rally to an English army; and if the British could hold the southern coast, they could strangle rebel commerce in that region, draining slaves and commodities away from the rich tidewater lands. In late December, 1778, the new strategy was launched with the seizure of Savannah in the Colony of Georgia. A new front had been opened in the war. In Nova Scotia, too, both rebels and royalists would change tactics and create new nightmares for one another in 1779. It would be a year of both new betrayals and 'déjà vu'.

# NIGHTMARES

BENEDICT ARNOLD: 'PATRIOT' Hero. Daring rebel commander with a reputation for personal courage and a very hot temper, not suffering fools lightly.

Benedict Arnold: Disgruntled, glory-seeking malcontent. A man bent on improving his social station, having convinced himself that lesser men had obtained higher rank and privilege while he was passed over without adequate reason or explanation.

Maybe both views held by those who knew him were correct. And because Arnold was so popular with the rebel mob, his betrayal in order to further his own standing and fortune was all the more keenly felt by Americans when that treason was publically revealed.

After the British evacuated Philadelphia in June, 1778, General Arnold was appointed military commander of the city by General Washington. He immediately sought to personally profit from his new position, not an unheard of endeavour among high-ranking military men, rebel or British. The 38 year old Arnold also found love with an 18 year old Peggy Shippen, daughter of a judge and 'loyalist' sympathizer. The two married (his second marriage) and lived extravagantly while Arnold grew exasperated with the economic state of the country, the prosecution of the war and alleged conspiracies against him, both real and imagined. He was also strongly opposed to the alliance with France and decried the rejection of British overtures to the rebels that Great Britain would allow the Americans full self-government under the Crown. He began to associate with several renowned 'loyalists' in Philadelphia, including a local Tory merchant who put him in contact with Jonathan Odell of New York- a person who would later play a prominent role in the politics of our region. Odell knew William Franklin, former Royal Governor of New Jersey, a 'loyalist' and, ironically, the son of prominent 'patriot', Benjamin Franklin. William Franklin, in turn, put Arnold in contact with British spies he knew, using Arnold's wife as an intermediary.

By July, 1779, General Arnold was secretly supplying important military information to the British under General Henry Clinton headquartered in the city of New York and was being well paid for it. Still, the always argumentative Arnold dickered over the terms of his service and overestimated his value to the British. At the same time he argued with the rebel authorities over money he supposedly owed to the Continental Congress and difficulties with his command in Philadelphia. In addition, Arnold was facing court-martial proceedings being brought against him by other rebel officers with whom he had served and frequently berated. By the end of the year he was very ill-disposed towards the rebel cause and was ready to make a full 'turn' towards the royalist side.

I spent much of the winter of 1778-1779 off hunting and trapping in the wilderness surrounding Chignecto. I accumulated lynx, marten, fox and even a few muskrat and much-valued beaver pelts, all of which I could trade for a healthy sum at Fort Cumberland or, come spring, to pelt traders who visited the Isthmus. The solitude of the hunt was also appealing: It gave me time to reflect, plan and reorganize my thoughts. But spending so much time in the freezing wilderness could also be dangerous: The stinging cold could be exceedingly painful, the snow deep, the ice treacherous and violent blizzards could blow in out of nowhere across the Great

Marsh. More than one hunter had become disoriented, lost and then froze to death on the marsh. On at least two occasions I was trapped in blizzards overnight and was forced to quickly build for myself temporary shelters in the snow and fires to warm those places, fending off the bite of the frost and allowing me a means to prepare several meals. Sitting in those shelters as the wind howled around me, my thoughts sometimes returned to the winter of 1751-1752 when I crisscrossed the countryside around Annapolis with Wilmot's Rangers. Those were such innocent times. Now I had to struggle with thoughts of a murdered wife, an injured son and the future of my household.

I really need not have worried about either my son or my household. Jonah recovered quickly, although without the use of his right arm. He learned to write and rely on his left side for most everything, and was assured by the lawyer Jackman in Halifax that there would always be a place for him as a clerk whenever he was prepared to take it up. This motivated Jonah to become as fit as his body would allow. Meanwhile, the other children stepped into the breach and assumed command of the running of the household. Mark took up masonry and carpentry with the White family, like Jonah before him, and continued working on 'Stonehaven Reborn' when I was not available to assist. Heather became matron of the house and learned to cook every manner of meal for the family while keeping our home clean and comfortable. Peter was an excellent farm labourer and tended to the crops and the livestock with great skill. I was proud of them all. I know that they mourned the loss of their mother but did not go about displaying it. Instead, they all contributed and did everything that they could to help me keep the household running smoothly. The Dixons offered me the use of their slave, Zipporah, to assist with the housework, but given the fact that my children were doing an admirable job and my long-standing opposition to involuntary servitude, I declined the offer without giving offence.

The war at sea reached new levels of savagery in late 1778 and early 1779. Many rebel crews acted more like actual pirates than privateers, stripping captured crews of their personal possessions, even down to their clothing. Those privateers simply divided up the spoils among themselves, never reporting their captures to rebel authorities. Canso was struck again by 'patriot' privateers and 50,000 pounds worth of damage was inflicted on our fishery. This prompted a kind of 'privateer fever' in Halifax with many Letters of Marque being issued by the authorities and local vessels being fitted out for the war, going by such names as the 'St. Mary's packet' and the 'Halifax Bob'. These marauders exacted a terrible revenge on rebel commerce and some of their military vessels, although both sides tried to keep the number of dead seamen to a minimum, choosing instead to incorporate captured and willing enemy sailors into their privateer crews and imprisoning the rest. Being at sea was certainly preferable to being in chains on a prison barge or in some dungeon carved out of rock on an island in Halifax Harbour. Rebel or royalist could not take great pride in the way prisoners-of-war were kept or treated during the American Rebellion.

One of the worst things one could be during these times was a 'neurtral': Neutrality simply opened a person up to abuses by both Crown and 'patriot'. If you were neutral, one party always assumed that you secretly supported the other. The fact that Nova Scotia had not declared for America caused privateers to suspect that the whole of the population were rabid 'loyalists'; yet any hesitation by a citizen to loudly proclaim his or her loyalty to the Crown rendered them 'secret rebels' in the eyes of the authorities. Many south shore families were robbed by the privateers because they supported the royalist side, then they were arrested by the royalists for being too accommodating to the privateers! Rebel Colonel John Allan, to his credit, saw the folly and abuse in these proceedings and advocated with Massachusetts to rein in the rebel privateers, but to no avail. The deprivations continued. Commodities such as pork, beef, flour, even hay, became scarce as the privateers squeezed the province.

Yarmouth was under a virtual blockade and its port nearly closed. Minas was raided. One lone privateer quickly inflicted 10,000 pounds damage on the economy by seizing various merchantmen. The military rushed to build new defenses and roads to speed their response to the privateers but the resulting taxes and levies to support these undertakings threatened to break an already struggling economy.

In May of 1779 I received word by way of a soldier from Fort Cumberland that a Mi'kmaq Indian named Nicholas had come into the fort asking to speak with me. I went up to the fort with pipes and some tobacco, found this Nicholas and took him aside for a smoke. He spoke good English and told me that he was a messenger sent by Gerome who wanted to inform me that 'Petite Copage' had gathered around him a contingent of followers who were preparing to drive the English from the Miramichi. The English settlers at that place were now very fearful and hoped for aid from the British authorities. The chiefs and headmen of the Mi'kmaq were also very concerned for they knew that such activity in the past had resulted in a new British fort and garrison being established in Maliseet territory-a consequence the Mi'kmaq wished to avoid at all costs. A great council was being called for the early summer in Miramichi to discuss all of this and wampum belts were now flying from village to village summoning important participants. Gerome did not know if young Copage's designs could be wholly defeated, but the British must know of the imminent danger.

I trusted this courier as he had certain information that only Gerome would have known. I thanked Nicholas and purchased a knife for him at the fort as a gift in appreciation. I told him to inform Gerome that I was very happy he saw fit to tell me these things, passed along out of friendship and concern, and that I would do all in my power to provide his family with some valuable presents at a later date in recognition of this fact. Nicholas agreed to carry back this message. I immediately went to see Lieutenant-Colonel Gorham. He was horrified at the prospect of a Mi'kmaq revolt on the Miramichi, that great waterway of the northeast. Such an uprising would put at risk the infant settlements around Miramichi Bay and up and down the lengths of the various branches of the Miramichi river system; but there were really no troops available to dispatch to that place or remain for an extended period of time unless there were some great rupture between the Mi'kmaq Nation as a whole and the English. He would send off my report to Halifax and request assistance and direction. He then asked me if I thought it worthwhile to bring together a small corps of 'rangers' to be ready to head to that northeastern 'tinder box' on a moment's notice. Of course, he also asked if I would lead such a force. As I was still his servant I had little choice but to agree. He asked me as well if I could prepare a list of men who might be suitable to serve with such a force, at least 20 strong. I told him I would create this inventory, but did not know where all of these men might be now, how they could be reached, or if they were even alive. He indicated that he would take care of those aspects as well as the provisioning of this group. Despite the fact that it might mean that I would be leaving my family once more, I thought Gorham's plan to be a good one and worthy of implementation. I prepared the list immediately and handed it over to Gorham.

In due course 'Hawkins' Rangers' was born: Some of the men were drawn from my list and were of the best quality, such as Nathan Spencer who I had served with in Wilmot's company during the French and Indian War, and with whom I shared a French prison at Québec in 1758-1759; others were less suitable, knowing little about military matters, let alone 'ranging', having hardly spent any time in the wilderness. Such was the case with a Mister Adam Beckwith who would later prove to be a problem for me. I enlisted all of the applying volunteers, however, at Gorham's insistence in order to quickly fill out my 20 man unit. Many of the men I had hoped to enlist for the rangers were now serving with other units or had been killed in this war or the last. Others had simply vanished, had died of natural causes or were too old to serve: Such was the case with Mister Dixon, a former member of Danks's Rangers, who I felt would provide better service watching over his farm and mine. I later learned that some of the urgency with which the ranger unit was being formed derived from the fact that Lieutenant-Colonel Gorham had received new reports of an increase in the number of rebel privateers cruising the Gulf of St. Lawrence for 'prizes' headed for Canada and, ominously, reports that French vessels were now observed sailing close to Miramichi Bay. John Allan's agents were also rumoured to be circulating among the Mi'kmaq. All of the elements for an explosion of rebel violence were present.

While the idea of a Mi'kmaq revolt was causing nightmares among British officials, the British were also planning to create nightmares for the rebels: It was decided at the highest levels in Great Britain that a new refuge was needed for fleeing New England 'loyalists' to be located somewhere along the coast of Maine. This new port could also serve as an interdiction station for the Royal Navy operating against rebel privateers who were ravaging the Nova Scotia coastline. It was finally decided that the best location for this base was the old French haunt of Castine or 'Bagaduce' in the District of Maine which, if successfully established, would create a 'buffer' province between Massachusetts and British Nova Scotia. Machias, which had proven to be too tough of a nut to crack for the British, would actually be isolated to the east of Castine. The new sanctuary for fleeing 'loyalists' would be called the province of 'New Ireland' and would technically embrace the area from the Saco River in the west to the St. Croix River in the east (although the British would never exercise real control over so large an area).The commander of British forces in America, General Clinton, ordered a naval force and army units under the command of General Francis McLean in Halifax to seize a proper site for a fort at Penobscot Bay near Castine. MacLean sailed to the area from Halifax on May 30, 1779, and arrived in Penobscot Bay on June 12th. He had 700 men with him: Engineers, artillerymen, troops from the 74th (Highland)

Regiment and soldiers from the 82nd Regiment. A place on a peninsula was selected for their new 'Fort George', exterior batteries were erected to protect the location and armed warships sat in the sheltered harbour nearby. My unit of rangers was almost assigned to the expedition sailing from Halifax to Castine but events in Miramichi intervened to prevent that redirection. Unfortunately, establishing a fort and garrison at Miramichi might have been a better use for some of the troops sent off to establish this new province isolated in the centre of coastal Maine.

The rebels reacted quickly to this British incursion into the very heart of a territory considered by the 'patriots' to be a sacred and inviolate part of Massachusetts. Should the British be able to hold Castine they might even convince the Penobscot Indian Nation to switch their allegiance to the Crown as the tribe had tended to favour the rebel side under the influence of Mister Allan. They had sometimes provided warriors for Allan's visits and raids to the St. John River. With a British fort at the mouth of the Penobscot River, choking off their seasonal access to the coast and trade with New England, the tribe might reconsider their rebel leanings. Meanwhile, Massachusetts requested and received naval help from the Continental Congress and mobilized 1000 militia plus artillery units to oust our forces. The rebel armada arrived on July 25th and, despite a good effort, their early attacks were repulsed. On July 28th the main assault was launched with 400 men-half Continental Marines, half militia. They drove British forces from a bluff under intense fire and the Marines in particular suffered heavy casualties. This led to a dispute between the naval and land force commanders over the best way to prosecute the siege. While a number of batteries changed hands repeatedly, there was no storming of the fort and the rebel navy seemed to hold back its support, reluctant to help the land forces or clash with the Royal Navy.

On August 12th a strong British naval relief force arrived from New York. The rebels were engaged and driven up the

Penobscot River where they were forced to scuttle much of their fleet. Their militia, regulars, Marines and remaining navy men (now on foot) struggled back through the wilderness to the territory still controlled by the rebels, suffering additional losses. 'New Ireland' had been saved. It survived the war and a few hundred "loyalists' did flock there. Its strategic location kept the Penobscot Indians 'neutral', if not decidedly in favour of England-which was more than acceptable to British officials. Royal Navy ships sailing from Castine were also able to operate quite successfully against rebel privateers. At war's end the British evacuated the place and many 'loyalists' moved to British controlled areas around Passamaquoddy Bay. 'New Ireland' then ceased to exist.

In the spring of 1779 'Petite Copage' was rallying his supporters at Miramichi. In a series of local councils he argued that if the Mi'kmaq drove the English from the northeast of Nova Scotia, the French would return, their friendship would be restored and a robust trade would follow. He outlined to his followers the series of abuses visited on the Mi'kmaq by the English: Being cheated in their trade; being pushed from the best hunting and fishing grounds by settlers; being denied gunpowder for their hunting; being looked down upon and treated shabbily by these newly arriving white men. He said it was time to take up the hatchet once again and force the English to retire. This need not be a full-scale war involving all of the Mi'kmaq in Nova Scotia, but the message had to be sent that the Miramichi was exclusive Mi'kmaq territory and no prior treaty gave the English the right to engage in such thefts and abuses. Even before the planned grand council among all the Mi'kmaq was held, 'Petite Copage' and his followers would strike. In May and early June, 1779, young Copage's warriors started to plunder English settlers and traders around Miramichi. This news quickly reached Lieutenant-Colonel Gorham at Fort Cumberland who immediately called together my rangers and dispatched them by land to the northeast, there being no armed sloops immediately available to carry us.

Gorham promised to send word to Halifax as soon as he could as to what was happening in Miramichi and he would try as best he could to support us. I hoped this was the case as we would be outnumbered ten to one by Mi'kmaq warriors. We started off with our provisions and canoes up the Petitcoudiac River, then by carrying places to a great lake in the centre of the region northwest of Chignecto. From there, an ample number of waterways allowed us to proceed northeast to Miramichi. But the water in the rivers and streams was sometimes too low for our canoes and we had to carry them. This was a wild country made up principally of vast forests, small and medium rivers and some mountainous areas. It was very rich in terms of wildlife, with moose, wolves, bear, and fish aplenty. But we could not hunt as we had to be careful not to give away our approach with the discharge of a musket. Our rangers could only be effective if no one knew of our presence.

As we came closer to Miramichi Bay we started to encounter fleeing settlers. They all had horror stories of being told to leave the region or die, much as the loyal settlers on the St. John River had been told the previous year. Men, women and children, sometimes with their old people, dogs and a few possessions were jammed into canoes and heading as quickly as possible towards the southwest. A few had been burned out and plundered. While they hoped for an avenging army to descend on Miramichi, they were shocked to find out that we were 'it'- 20 men for now. They continued on their way while we kept moving to the northeast. One particular group of settlers stopped us and told us that they were being pursued by Mi'kmaq warriors and that we should intervene and stop them. I found it unusual that the Mi'kmaq would come this far south after a few fleeing settlers, but I told them that we would make some observations. The leader of this group, a Mister Liam Murphy, said incredulously, "You better damn well do more than just 'observe', before we all end up dead." I told him not to worry and to proceed on his way. We went a little further up the river, found a good observation point on a small cliff close to the water, hid ourselves in the surrounding trees, and then waited.

By and by, two canoes of Indians were seen paddling down the river. I studied them closely. They were not Mi'kmaq at all, but Maliseet hunters with their families. I whispered to the men to simply hold their fire and let them pass. Mister Beckwith, who knew nothing of Indians, nervously insisted that we should kill them all. I told him to stand down. He said, "You are just going to let those murderers escape and overtake that settler family?" I told him once more to stand down. I could see him bringing his musket up to the firing position. I quickly grabbed up my hatchet and put it to his neck saying, "If you take that shot, I will take your head." He immediately lowered his weapon. The Maliseet went on their way. I then explained to the group why I had done what I had done. I also told them that we were only going to survive if my orders were strictly observed. Any man that could not follow this requirement should return to Fort Cumberland now, for if I was disobeyed in the field I planned to kill the man who challenged me. That seemed to set things right.

We finally reached Miramichi Bay. On the bay, there were a considerable number of Mi'kmaq canoes heading north along the coast. It had to be time for the grand council of which Gerome had sent word. We followed the canoes but initially set up our camp at a spot far enough removed from any council site that we would not be discovered. As soon as we made our camp I decided to go out on a scout to see what I could find. I kept moving to the north along the coast and near a small cove I found a French frigate at anchor. It was ferrying muskets, gunpowder and supplies ashore to waiting Mi'kmaq. There were two French officers moving about near the landing place. It seemed that they were also utilizing a log cabin built on a bluff overlooking the cove. One French soldier was standing guard there. This might be an interesting site to visit, come evening. I went back to our camp and talked with Mister Spencer and a Mister Riley Henson (who had proven quite capable so far on this mission) about my plan. They did not hesitate to agree to accompany me back to the cabin at night.

As the sun went down, the fog rolled in and it was difficult to make our way. We finally found the cabin and crept close to it. There was no guard. Two French voices could be heard inside. I told Spencer, "We will rush them and see what we can find. Do not hesitate. Kill them if you must. I am as interested in documents as I am in any prisoners." Given that we were such a small force, prisoners would be a burden to us, but we would take away any Frenchmen who were quick to surrender. While Henson stood watch outside, Spencer and I burst through the door to confront the two surprised Frenchmen. One lurched forward for a pistol on a table in front of him. Spencer hurled his hatchet and struck that Frenchman square in the head, killing him; but the other French officer, in full uniform, turned quickly and was able to exit a door facing the cove. I knew him as soon as I saw him: It was Lieutenant Andre' who I had met on my arrival in Nova Scotia in 1751, and then several times thereafter, including at Québec in 1758-1759 (although it seems he had risen in rank since the last time I encountered him, probably to the French equivalent of a Major).

I had a loaded pistol and assumed that he was heading for the French frigate through some brush along a rough and treacherous trail leading to the cove. I followed. It was dark and quite foggy, yet a ghostly moon shone through, giving some light. The air was clammy. It was deathly quiet. Suddenly, there stood Andre', like some form of spectre, with a cocked pistol pointed towards me. I reacted quickly and cocked my own weapon, pointing it directly at him.

He said," Hello Mister Hawkins, fancy meeting you here."

I said, "I was just as surprised to make your acquaintance. What are you doing here? You should be in France."

He said, "I am here doing the bidding of my King, as always. I assume you are doing the same. My superiors seem to think I know a thing or two about this country. Now rather than shoot you, I would much prefer that you simply let me make it to my ship where I will then advise our Captain to weigh anchor and sail away. My business here is done. There is no reason for us to kill one another."

Trying to sound menacing, I said, "You know I cannot let you leave. You are a spy operating in His Majesty's province. You will have to come back with me and tell my superiors exactly what you know and what your countrymen have been up to."

He smiled and said,"You know I cannot go with you. I am no spy. I am in full uniform serving our allies, the Mi'kmaq, in their sovereign territory. Your actions remind me of what your Governor Cornwallis did with our vessel back in 1751. Now, before my finger twitches and the hammer falls on this pistol, you are going to allow me to disappear into the fog and be seen no more. It will be as if I never existed." He started backing up.

I yelled "HALT!" but he just kept retreating. I wanted to fire but could not bring myself to do it. Shooting him would be like destroying a cherished part of my own past. Finally his image melted into the fog. Just as in 1754 at Lawrence Town, I hesitated and allowed him to escape. I went back to the cabin. Spencer and Henson were going through a treasure-trove of documents. "It seems to me that there has been a lot of secret French and rebel activity occurring in these parts," Spencer said. "What happened to the other Frenchie?" he asked.

"I lost him in the fog" I said.

The next morning, our rangers broke camp and continued to head north towards the possible site of the Mi'kmaq council. To make our way we simply had to follow a new flotilla of canoes that were heading north. When we reached the council site I found a secluded, elevated position from which we could watch the proceedings. The council was being held near the mouth of a river a short distance from where the bay widened to meet the Gulf of St Lawrence. The council was guarded by heavily armed warriors. The principle men sat in a half-circle and listened intently to the representations. As before, 'Petite Copage' interrupted many of these solemn addresses, much to the annoyance of his seated elders. I could see Gerome and he would sometimes get up and walk away from the council when Copage was speaking. Ominously, a sloop of war flying the rebel flag suddenly appeared off the coast in full view of the assembly. Copage became jubilant and kept pointing in the direction of the sloop as if to say, "See, our friends have come to help us." A boat was launched from the vessel and it flew a large French flag, which caused some excitement among the council's members.

Then a mortar bomb came screaming ashore and exploded against a tree near the council.

A red-hot piece of shrapnel passed directly through 'Petite Copage', front to back, killing him instantly. A second bomb also streaked in and exploded near the council, killing another participant, wounding and scattering many more. The long boat that approached the coast carried British Marines. The rebel flag and the French colours were merely a ruse to allow the Marines to get in close without taking fire. They charged from the landing place with fixed bayonets into the council area and seized a dozen or more prisoners, some wounded. More boatloads of Marines followed. We broke out of our concealment and went down to assist the Marines, who seemed genuinely surprised that we were even in the area. At first, of course, they were a bit concerned that we were rebels playing at being the King's rangers but I showed their commander my written orders from Lieutenant-Colonel Gorham and detailed our progress to date. Convinced of our authenticity, the Marine lieutenant directed our attention to the commander of the sloop 'Viper', a Mister Hervey, who was still offshore.

Gerome spied me and came to talk with me. We embraced and exchanged pleasantries. He then asked if I could introduce the Chief of the Miramichi Indians to the master of the sloop 'Viper' in order that they might reach some accommodation, especially with respect to the Mi'kmaq who had been seized. I said I would do my best and took from my supplies several items to give to Gerome in the form of presents that I had promised him through the messenger, Nicholas. Gerome expressed his thanks and indicated that the majority of the council's members were strongly opposed to any war with the English. As we were in the district of Miramichi, the Chief of that area, John Julian, could be expected to speak for the rest. I asked Gerome to go and fetch Julian and I would take him to Captain Hervey. Gerome secured the Chief, and with the help of the Marine commander and his men, we all went out to the 'Viper'. Captain Hervey was attentive while listening to Gerome's translation. Hervey indicated that while he could do nothing about the prisoners at this point in time, given his orders, he was prepared to sign an interim treaty with Chief Julian and treat the prisoners with the utmost care and respect. Though disappointed, Julian agreed to Hervey's offer and waited while the terms of the agreement were drawn up on parchment. The document was simply a reaffirmation of Mi'kmaq loyalty to the Crown and a promise not to molest any of the English settlers or traders. To go beyond such a certification of loyalty and promise of peaceable behavior would not be within Hervey's mandate: Michael Francklin would have to be involved with anything more extensive. The document was translated through the efforts of Gerome and I. Julian signed the treaty and indicated that the British could expect peace going forward, but it was important that the Mi'kmaq who were taken, some of whom were important figures among that tribe, be well treated.

In due course, I bid farewell to Gerome, collected up my rangers and was taken by the 'Viper' to Green Bay across the Isthmus of Chignecto from Fort Cumberland. The sloop then took the Indian prisoners on to Québec. We had done all that our small force was tasked with doing, mainly protecting settlers we came across; gathering information about French, rebel and Mi'kmaq intentions; helping to bring about a peace. For now, it looked like the revolt on the Miramichi was over, but a lot would depend on how the Indian prisoners fared and when they would be released. It did not take long for the prisoners to be transferred from Québec to Halifax. In September of 1779, Indian Superintendent Michael Franklin summoned the Mi'kmaq headman representing their districts from the Bay de Chaleurs in the north to Cape Tormentine, near Chignecto, in the south to come to Fort Edward at Minas and conclude a proper treaty.

I was later told that the Mi'kmaq treaty of September, 1779, was not that different from other treaties I had occasion to observe going back to 1752. The Indians promised to protect the persons and property of English settlers and traders, report on any conspiracies among those Indians who may be inclined against the British and that they would ratify and confirm all treaties with the Crown going back to Governor Lawrence's time (the early 1760's). They also agreed to break all ties with John Allan and any other rebels or enemies of the Crown (that is, the French). In return, Francklin promised the Mi'kmaq, as the Crown's representative, "That the said Indians and their constituents shall remain in the districts before mentioned, quiet and free from any molestation of any of his Majesty's troops or other good subjects in their hunting and fishing" and were told that honest traders would be sent among them to provide them with all they may want in terms of necessaries for the winter. The usual presents were distributed and I was told that the Mi'kmaq delegation, led by John Julian, went away fairly well satisfied. The Indian prisoners were released in October after swearing an Oath of Allegiance to the King. Another clash with an Indian Nation was avoided through a judicious application of promises, presents, violence and threats of future violence.

As the fall of the year approached, our efforts on the farm increased to bring in a harvest and prepare for the long winter ahead, especially with Gisèle gone and Jonah maimed; but we somehow managed. Jonah informed me that this would be his last year at 'Stonehaven Reborn' as (with my permission, of course) his plan was to begin clerking for Mister Jackman in Halifax in the spring. Mister Jackman had managed to find him a room where Jonah could board at a home owned by a fine family which, by all accounts, was not far from where a Colonel Johnston I had once met had lived. I told him that I would try and arrange his passage on a sloop out of Fort Lawrence Landing by spring and would send him off with the few pence (and no doubt pounds) that I could scape together to help establish him in Halifax.

I was happy to see that he would be fulfilling his dream: This achievement would be the best testament to his mother, who had taught him well and would have been exceedingly proud of him. Maybe our year of nightmares was finally over. It was high time for new beginnings.

# BEGINNINGS

$F$EBRUARY, 1780. THE British continued to pursue their 'southern strategy', and this resulted in a decisive victory for our side. Generals Clinton and Cornwallis evacuated Newport, Rhode Island, (which the British held since late 1776) and moved all of those forces against Charles Town in the Carolinas, landing near that city in early February. The British quickly pulled a tight siege around that rebel-held location by April 1st, and they were assisted in that endeavor by the former Lieutenant-Governor (really, the former acting-Governor) of Nova Scotia, Marriot Arbuthnot, now in command of the force's naval arm. The rebel governor fled; the principal fortification, Fort Moultrie, surrendered; by early May the British were lobbing heated shot into the city, creating a firestorm. Charles Town was surrendered by the rebels on May 12th. Over 3000 prisoners were taken, although only 100-odd men on each side were killed in the preceding battles. The British captured huge quantities of ordnance, cannons, tents, muskets, gunpowder, ships and wagons within or near the city. The surrender was the largest rebel capitulation to date and a serious blow to the 'patriot' cause in the south. General Clinton left for New York and General Cornwallis was in command at Charles Town.

The British plan was, with 'loyalist' help, to spread the Crown's influence throughout the southern colonies, much like spilled ink spreading out over paper. Unfortunately, the extent of available 'loyalist' assistance was greatly overestimated from the very beginning, as was the likelihood that the 'patriots', especially those in the backcountry, would ever meekly submit to a newly imposed British rule. British forts and coastal cities became enclaves where the 'loyalists' flocked for protection and devoured supplies. Those places ended up being surrounded by rebels utilizing 'hit-and-run' ranger style tactics. The fight degenerated into a particularly vicious one: While most of the major battles were won by our forces, the rebels still roamed freely throughout the countryside, striking at our supply trains, isolated garrisons and the rearguards of British columns. Both sides allowed their base instincts to take control and atrocities were committed all around: prisoners were butchered, towns burned and innocents murdered, by both sides.

On January 15, 1780, the port of Halifax celebrated the news of the success of our forces against a determined rebel and French attack on Savannah in the Colony of Georgia. On the 18th the town had occasion to celebrate again when Queen Charlotte's birthday was honoured with lively festivities. Salutes, volleys and cannonades were delivered on both dates by the troops and 'ships of the line' in the harbour. For the Queen's birthday there was a Grand Ball and Supper held at the Pontack Inn, a location I sometimes frequented during my French and Indian War days. The Army and Royal Navy brought both protection and enterprise to Halifax, but there were sometimes problems: For instance, on the night of January 9th, three soldiers from a provincial regiment broke into a private home, stabbed the owner, fractured the skull of his lady guest, committed a robbery and then set fire to the place. They were quickly discovered by the authorities, tried and two of the three culprits executed. There were certainly 'two sides of the coin' to having large numbers of military men billeted in and around Halifax on a regular basis. While vast sums were made by merchants provisioning the troops and sailors, the town was forced to suffer through several ugly riots and material destruction at night initiated by drunken soldiers and navy men leaving parties held in their honour around the provincial capital.

1780 might easily be called the 'Year of the Privateer' in Nova Scotia, for not only did many more provincial vessels take to the sea to challenge rebel raiders, but coastal communities had finally learned to better assume control over their own defence. At both Lunenburg and the more westerly settlement of La Have local residents and militia were able to seize American privateers who arrived to take advantage of them. Rumours of a French 'armada' at sea also resulted in Halifax calling out the town and county militias and there was a strengthening of the port's fortifications, but no armada ever stopped by. There was a brief lull in the persistent privateer attacks on the province as a result of the establishment of the Royal Navy base at Penobscot: Rebel losses as a result of the naval fight at that place were enormous, including fifteen of their best privateers. Additional rebel resources were drained away in a belated and unsuccessful effort to resupply the 'patriot' forces near Penobscot. Machias, the former privateer haven, was under blockade by the Royal Navy. Now, it was Massachusetts communities that felt the sting of royalist privateers. Nova Scotia enjoyed the respite while it lasted. Goods flowed in from Great Britain once again easing the shortage of supplies.

Not all sea tales were as heroic as our efforts at coastal defence and privateering: In February, 1780, the New York-bound schooner 'Freemason' ran aground near Canso and only three of her 20-man crew managed to survive in the coastal wilderness. Unfortunately, their survival came about mostly through Cannibalism, with the survivors feasting on the bodies of the dead. No doubt those three men would live with the shame of their actions for many years to come. Most sailors could not conceive of resorting to such desperate measures in times of emergency, even as a result of a shipwreck; but, of course, one must actually be in those circumstances in order to make an informed choice. Another not-so-savoury aspect of life at sea was the practice of random men becoming the object of the roving eyes of 'press gangs' used by the Royal Navy to fill its depleted ranks. Private sailors-fishermen, merchantmen, privateers-were prized candidates and sought out by these gangs, then lured into dark alleyways in Halifax with promises of drink, women or money. They were beaten half-senseless and 'pressed' into service with His Majesty's Navy. The victims might not see home or family again for many years to come and, of course, risked being killed during storms, falling from the masts or rigging, or in sea battles with the rebels or the French. The 'gangs' became so commonplace and brutal that there were protests and riots by area seamen on the Halifax wharves who were opposed to the practice. Even a man of my age was not immune from being 'pressed' into the naval service. One had to be on guard in a port like Halifax. I always carried a hunting knife in my boot, Highland style, just in case I ever encountered such kidnappers.

In May, 1780, Jonah prepared to leave Chignecto to read the law with the lawyer, Mister Jackman, in Halifax. We loaded up our oxcart with his baggage and as his siblings cried we held what amounted to a brief ceremony to send him off on his way. He gave his horse over to Mark, asking him to take good care of it and to check in on the welfare of Anna Chapman whenever he could, and with whom Jonah would be regularly corresponding. Jonah and I left the home that he had helped to build, and rebuild, and headed for Fort Lawrence Landing to catch the sloop which I had arranged to take him to Halifax. He was both nostalgic and excited as we made the trip to the Landing. After his things were loaded on the vessel and his passage paid, I bid him a final farewell, hugged him, told him how proud I was of him and reiterated how proud his mother would have been of him. I told him that I would make every effort to visit him soon. I stood at the Landing for a long time watching the sails of the sloop depart to the west. I was missing him already.

And 'Hawkins' Rangers' were no more. Lieutenant-Colonel Gorham and the Fencibles were ordered to abandon Fort Cumberland and return to Halifax. The place had apparently outlived its usefulness. As a consequence of the withdrawal, our rangers in general, and me more specifically, were seen as an unnecessary expense and struck from the rolls. I said goodbye to Gorham and the many friends I had made in the ranks of the Fencibles. They had all done an admirable job and, I believe, did much to save the province from the rebels. A few retired soldiers, Mister Dixon included, were tasked with keeping up the buildings, casement's and ramparts of the fort as best they could in order to prevent the type of ruin that had befallen the place prior to 1776. Gunpowder and some arms would still be kept there for the benefit of the militia and the place was seen as a possible 'forward redoubt' for the Army should any rebels arrive once again in the area north of Chignecto. As the retired men were paid only a small stipend to keep the place in good repair not much work was really done towards that end. Soon this site of two significant British victories-one in this war, and one in the last- was allowed to go to seed. It would be some time before the place became of any real use to the Crown again, other than as a storage place for ordnance. And with the dissolution of the rangers I no longer had the luxury of my Army pay to fall back on.

With the theatre of war having shifted to the south, the British government was intent on finding ways to save money now that there was stalemate in the north. One of the areas where it was thought expenses could be trimmed was with respect to the Indian Nations. The days of winning the favour of the tribes with extensive presents and supplies were over-at least as far as the government in London was concerned. General Clinton was ordered to keep a lid on Indian expenditures in the northern theatre and he exerted the authority of the military over the Indian Superintendents to accomplish that end. This approach horrified Michael Francklin who had taken great care to develop what he believed to be a very prudent approach to ensuring Indian neutrality. He prayed that his strategy, so carefully crafted over time, would not now be quickly blasted by 'penny-pinchers'. He invested some of his own funds in the Indian Superintendent's Office to ensure that basic expenditures were still being met and began begging the Lord's in London for at least a minimal flow of financial support. He had some limited success, but it was always a close-run thing and subject to significant opposition, especially from the generals.

In January, 1780, Benedict Arnold came out of his court-martial with convictions for only two relatively minor infractions. Still, he was seriously rebuked by General Washington, and the Continental Congress continued to pursue him for 1000 pounds he allegedly owed them for expenditures made during the Québec campaign. Furious over the rebuke and the fact that much of his paperwork for the expenditures had been lost in the retreat from Québec, Arnold made a show of resigning his Philadelphia command in late April, 1780. Still, some of Arnold's rebel friends sought out other important command positions for him, including the possibility that he might become principal officer at a key rebel bastion called, ironically, Fort Arnold at West Point, New York, on the Hudson River. This post helped to control traffic on the Hudson and keep the British to the north in Canada from uniting with General Clinton's forces at New York. Benedict Arnold made his British spy friends aware of the possibility of the new command and provided them with what information he could on the post and how it could be delivered into their hands without an assault. He also increased the price of his cooperation with the Crown to in excess of 20,000 pounds, plus the payment of other expenses he owed or allegedly owed.

On August 3, 1780, Arnold got his command at West Point. General Clinton then agreed to most (but not all) of Arnold's extravagant blackmail. An important meeting about to take place between Arnold and the British on the Hudson River aboard the vessel HMS 'Vulture' in order to finalize these arrangements was interrupted by rebel land-based cannon fire that drove off the British warship. A series of conflicting and untimely messages then flew between Arnold and his spy contacts; but those incriminating communications were intercepted and the spies were arrested by the rebels. Arnold had to flee to the 'Vulture' to be spirited away. The 'turn' from rebel to royalist was now fully complete, but thereafter Benedict Arnold was vilified (and almost kidnapped) by the rebels and was never particularly well liked or trusted by the British authorities. It was an enormous and tragic fall from grace.

Determined to see that the peace he had helped to establish with the Maliseet and Mi'kmaq did not unravel, Michael Francklin organized a new congress with those tribes on the St. John River in mid-June, 1780. Major Studholme attended in Francklin's place and oversaw it all. More than 1000 Indians came to the council, including deputies from the Ottawa, Huron, Algonkian and Abenaki Nations in Canada. The British objective was to have those deputies threaten the tribes of Nova Scotia that if they did not totally withdraw from the rebel side they would be treated as enemies of the Indians of Canada. As a result of those threats (and a promise of more presents) most of the remaining warriors at Machias withdrew back into Nova Scotia. The British hoped that the old 'Wabanaki' Confederacy, which had been formed among the Indian Nations of Maine and Nova Scotia and had supported the French in the last war, would somehow evolve into part of a new British-supported alliance of tribes from across the north and northeast opposed to the rebels. This was hoping for too much: While the Indian Nations of Nova Scotia may not be prepared to challenge the stronger tribes in Canada, they were also not prepared to take up the hatchet against the rebels. They returned to the form of quiet 'neutrality' which they had practised at the beginning of the American Rebellion. The rebels tried desperately to reverse this state of affairs, enticing the St. John's Indians and the Mi'kmaq with a French priest and other 'French gentlemen' (French traders and suppliers) established at Machias, but seemingly to no end. Michael Franklin was, once again, largely triumphant although he ended up 900 pounds in personal debt by year's end in his efforts to keep the Nova Scotia Indians peaceful.

By June I was able to arrange my affairs so that I could head off to Halifax to see how Jonah was doing. The Dixons again agreed to watch over 'Stonehven', although my children could now operate the place pretty much on their own. I secured a sturdy canoe, sufficient supplies and headed off down the La Planche trail into the heart of the peninsula of Nova Scotia. I turned west until I reached the coast, following an old French route once used to bring their soldiers and Indian allies on raids into the more settled parts of the province. I crossed over the Minas Basin and reached Fort Edward. From there it was on to the trail from the Acadian heartland to Halifax- a route where I was ambushed in 1751 while making a journey with Wilmot's Rangers; but I soon took to a chain of lakes and waterways which brought me right down to the edge of Halifax Harbour. I crossed over the harbour and finally arrived at Halifax proper. I pulled up my canoe at a convenient cove I knew from my old days at that place and started into town. It was not the Halifax I remembered from the 1750s. While the waterfront was still a rough and rowdy area, just as soon as you started moving west into the centre of the town the place had taken on a very refined appearance, with some carefully manicured streets and grand homes for the merchants, gentry and Crown officials. Whores and beggars were not as visible as in the early days. The population and number of buildings had increased dramatically. The military presence seemed to have insulated the capital from the terrible economic conditions found elsewhere in the province. And what we used to call 'Fort George' was now gone, as well as the forts and log palisades which once encircled the whole town. The new fortification at the top of the hill, near to where a previously unnamed fort once stood (which we in the military always called 'Fort George' out of respect for our King, George II), was simply referred to now as the 'Citadel'. It featured extensive earthworks, a log palisade wall and, at its centre, stood a large three-level 'blockhouse' with fourteen guns and capable of housing over 100 men. Other batteries within this secure fort mounted sufficient firepower to keep the Royal Navy anchorage quite safe.

I took a rented room above the 'Golden Ball' tavern near to the Pontack. Once I was settled I hurried to Mister Jackman's law chambers on Hollis Street. It was on Hollis Street that Brigadier-General Wolfe once resided both before and after the Louisbourg expedition. I arrived in the late afternoon just in time to catch Jonah before he left the office for the day. He was surprised and overjoyed to see me. We chatted for a while sitting on a bench near the street and I promised him a meal at the Pontack around 7 o'clock that evening. We walked about and he showed me the house where he was residing. He seemed happy with that arrangement. I returned to the 'Golden Ball' to wash and change into clothes more befitting a townsperson than a man emerging from the wilderness.

We had a fine meal at the Pontack that evening, which was an establishment even more elegant, lavish and elaborate than when I first spent time in Halifax. I noticed that Jonah still struggled while eating with his left hand but he did not complain. He seemed to have come to terms with his infirmity. We retired after the meal to a parlour for drinks. It was there over some brandy that our conversation turned to more serious topics.

"Why do you think my mother was killed?" Jonah asked.

I pondered the question for a moment then replied, "It was not your mother that Pierre Arsenault wanted dead, but me. Your mother simply got in the way. Arsenault panicked and shot her when she rushed to our door to warn me."

Jonah then replied, "And why did he want you dead?"

I said, "Hard feelings from the last war. Revenge, although Arsenault was much too young to have fully felt the worst atrocities visited on his people. But, of course, those were your mother's people as well and she suffered greatly from the harm inflicted on the Acadians by the English. We must not forget that it was a very brutal war. Terrible things were done to all sides-French, Indian and English. Arsenault no doubt grew up on horrific tales of the war and its effect on the Acadians at the feet of his elders. His honour demanded that he do something in reply. That 'something' was to kill an English ranger, and that would be me."

Jonah then asked, "Did you ever do things in this war or the last of which you were ashamed?"

I replied, "I destroyed property that I wished I had never destroyed. And I killed men in battle who I probably need not to have killed. But others I killed for they wished me dead and they tried very hard to make that wish a reality. I had no choice. 'Kill or be killed', as they say. I never inflicted harm-other than material harm-on the civilian population, never tortured a man or took a scalp. Did I fight a 'clean' war? There is no such thing. But I did what I could do so that I could live with myself."

Jonah seemed to accept my explanation. This was the closest I ever came to fully revealing what I had done during my war years, omitting the fact that I had murdered Captain Delahunt of my former ship, the 'Providence', out of rage and revenge, and that I had killed Alfred Weems as he was attacking Gisèle. These men were not casualties of war, however, but simply of my anger. My destruction of Acadian property, too, probably led to wintertime deaths that I put far out of my mind. But the face that haunted me the most in my dreams was that of a French officer that I killed outside of Louisbourg during an ambush by our rangers. I drove my bayonet straight through him while he stood there already staggered by a fatal wound. He looked to be in a state of shock, yet rather than assist him, I killed him as calmly and coolly as if he was just a beast in the forest. It was probably an unnecessary, senseless killing and I had yet to come to terms with it.

On July 10, 1780, I was still in Halifax, simply passing the time and walking about, when noise and confusion drew my attention to the waterfront. A crowd had gathered on a wharf not far from the site of the old 'Spread Eagle' Public House and they were pointing in the direction of Sambro Island at the mouth of the harbour where a lighthouse stood that guarded the harbour's entrance. Cannon fire could be heard coming from that direction but it was difficult to see exactly what was happening at a distance. A fisherman in the crowd who owned a small ketch cried out, "Who wants a closer look? Come on boys!" With that invitation a group of us crowded into his vessel and headed out towards the Sambro Light.

The fishing Captain had a glass which we passed around so that we could get a closer look at unfolding events. As we headed towards the lighthouse, it soon became apparent that two ships were locked in a close-quarters battle. When we were finally able to make out the vessels the Captain yelled, "IT IS OUR BRIG, THE RESOLUTION, AND A REBEL PRIVATEER, THE VIPER." The two ships were pounding each other, their cannons almost touching. Masts were collapsing, wood was splintering off the hulls, fires burned and crew members could be seen jumping into the sea from both vessels. The cannonade must have lasted almost two hours. Finally, we could make out the rebels storming our brig in a hail of musket fire and bomb-throwing. When it was all over the rebel ship was victorious and took the 'Resolution' as its 'prize'; but we learned later that 33 rebels died in the battle as opposed to 18 of our sailors, privateers all. We picked up some of the survivors, rebel and British, who were in the water and returned them dockside. I said a silent prayer for the lost sailors from both sides, having been a man of the sea myself once upon a time. Our boys got to 'privateer' another day; the rebels were marched off as prisoners to the 'Citadel'. Jonah did not get to see the fight as he was clerking, but I gave him a 'blow-by-blow' account when we met that evening for another round of dining at the Pontack.

It was mid-summer and time for me to leave town. It was going to be a long journey back home. Before packing up my things I went to see Jonah at Mister Jackman's law chambers one last time. I told him that I would try to come and see him again the next spring, and I gave him some extra money to help him get through the remaining months. As we talked, there was a good deal of activity going on around us. Two gentlemen had come into the office to sign some documents relating to their business dealings. Mister Jackman, leaning over a table in the common area, was making some notes. Jonah and I were nearby, saying our farewells.

Jackman said to one of the gentlemen, "Well Mister Perkins, one of our clerks will have the remainder of your documents prepared by tomorrow noon. Then we can proceed."

The gentleman replied, "Fine, that should give us plenty of time to complete the transaction, provided you do not have the 'cripple' over there prepare the papers for us," pointing to Jonah and laughing. Jackman let his mouth fall open, obviously not knowing what to say in reply.

Overhearing this, I angrily intervened. "You, sir, will immediately apologize to both Mister Jackman and his clerk, my son, for your verbal slight. My son, Jonah, is no 'cripple' and if the truth be known is probably more of a man than you will ever be," I said.

The gentleman, Mister Perkins, was astonished and shot back immediately, "You forget yourself you low-born bastard. I cannot believe that you dared to speak to me in that fashion. Do you know who I am? I own half this town. If you were a gentleman I would challenge you to a duel and obtain satisfaction."

I replied, "I could care less who you are or what you own, other than I know you are an ignorant fool. Do not let my station prevent you from seeking your satisfaction – unless you are a coward. I will fight you whenever, wherever, and in whatever manner you suggest."

Perkins smirked and said, "Good enough then. It will be with pistols, which I will provide. My second will be Mister Charles Cadbury here. I am thinking dawn tomorrow at Black Rock beach near Point Pleasant." I replied, "Fair enough, provided I can inspect the pistols, ammunition and conduct a 'test fire' before we duel. My son will be my second."

Perkins looked incredulous and said, "Fine. Inspect away and do what you like. The result will be the same. You will be a dead man or badly maimed. Do you really know what you are getting into? You do not look like a man skilled in the gentlemanly arts."

I said, "I do know what I am getting into and I have skills in a few 'arts' you have probably never explored." Perkins and Cadbury departed, laughing all the while.

Mister Jackman warned me later, "Mister Hawkins, that Perkins fellow has challenged a number of men in this town and has fought several successful duels at the location he indicated to you. We can still send word to him that you misspoke and now apologize for any insult he may have perceived, if you wish to avoid this unnecessary combat."

I said, "Why would I do that? It seems to me that Perkins needs to learn what being a 'gentleman' is all about. I did not come all the way to this province and make it my home just to be ordered about and subjected to insults by the likes of him. Only one of us will leave Black Rock beach tomorrow unscathed, and I intend it to be me."

Jonah was not pleased with my decision to duel. Even though he knew that I had served in two wars he also knew that any fight has an element of uncertainty that cannot be controlled. He begged me to reconsider so that he and the other children would not be left orphans. I reassured him that the odds were very much in my favour and that he and the children were well positioned for the future should things go awry; however, I meant what I said to Mister Jackman.

Jackman kindly accompanied Jonah and I to the duel site as it was not a location with which I was familiar from my early days in Halifax. We followed a winding trail through the forest leading to the sea, arriving at Black Rock, a craggy sand and pebble beach where public hangings were sometimes conducted or pirate corpses left to rot as a warning sign to others. We arrived at dawn. Perkins and Cadbury were late and smelled of rum. They looked like they had been up drinking all night and seemed a bit surprised that we were even there. They were accompanied by a Surgeon, a Mister Godfrey, I think. They walked right past us without saying a word, with Cadbury sticking cavalry sabres in the ground at select points to mark the proper distance between Perkins and I. Cadbury finally came to us with the chest containing a pistol and balls, and he furnished me with a pouch of powder which I stuck in my vest pocket. I 'test fired' the weapon and it worked admirably, although it was much smaller and lighter than any one of my own pistols at home.

Cadbury indicated, "When I drop my handkerchief you will advance towards Mister Perkins, and he towards you, firing and reloading at will until one or the other of you is dead or calls for a halt." He asked if I was now prepared to apologize to Mister Perkins and we could all walk away from this thing with our honour intact.

I said, in rather dramatic fashion, "Never".

Perkins looked wobbly. I was as much worried that he would shoot himself as he would me. Finally he stood with his pistol pointed towards the sky beside a sabre sticking in the ground. I did likewise. He cried out, "LET US UNLEASH HELL THEN."

Jonah asked, "Are you certain of this?" I replied, "Very." Mister Cadbury, standing halfway between us, dropped his handkerchief. Perkins and I started to advance towards one another. He fired his pistol almost immediately, hitting a tree to my left; then he started to reload, shaking all the while. In a few paces I was at a good range, factored the wind and what the pistol ball would do. I fired. Perkins was hit in the upper left shoulder, spinning him around, sending him to the ground and forcing him to drop his pistol out of sheer anguish.

I took out some powder from my vest pocket, calmly reloaded and walked over to him. Cadbury was yelling, "NO, NO, NO!" I was standing over Perkins and brought the pistol's hammer to 'full cock'. "Now sir, APOLOGIZE" I yelled.

He looked up at the pistol barrel pointed directly at his head and hastily said, "ENOUGH! I YIELD! I am sorry for what I said and that you, your son and Mister Jackman took offense. That was not my intention and I heartily apologize to everyone."

I fired my pistol into the air, looked down at him and said, "Good enough then. Apology accepted. Be mindful the next time you think of calling someone a 'cripple' or any other demeaning title." Then I yelled to his second, "GET THIS MAN A SURGEON AND PLENTY OF RUM."

Jackman, Jonah and I left the field and returned to town. I repeated my goodbyes, gathered up my things at the 'Golden Ball' and headed to the cove to retrieve my canoe. As was customary at that place, my boat had not been touched and sat there undisturbed among several other canoes, some of them of obvious Mi'kmaq manufacture. Soon I was paddling my way home up the lakes. Travelling through the wilderness, alone with my thoughts, I began to wonder if I was much too quick to take offense from Perkins. Had I sought out a confrontation? Was 'anger' my real problem, not idiots such as Perkins? No, I decided, there had to be 'boundaries', rules. If society and the law did not hold men like Delahunt, Weems, Arsenault and Perkins to account then someone must. 'Ranger Justice': I still lived by that Code. Sometimes evil men just had to be stopped, permanently. Justice was swift in wartime. It was still difficult to adjust to the slow pace, realities and rules of peacetime.

I arrived at home just in time to help with the harvest. Mark, with assistance from Peter, had made remarkable progress on the house, to the point that "Stonehaven" was fully 'Reborn'. Now we had to continue to refurnish the place and make it even more livable.

The first Sunday after my return, we all went up to 'Memerancook' together as a family to visit Gisèle's grave. The visitation caused the children to break down and weep uncontrollably, but I believe that it helped them with their healing. We bought and placed a new, more permanent grave marker in remembrance. Still, there were just too many '…what ifs…' that lingered: What if I had insisted on Arsenault being let go from our service before any violence erupted? What if I had tried to take Arsenault unawares from the rear of our house rather than through the front door? What if I had first tried to call him out into our front yard to face me? The speculation was endless, maddening and none of it brought back Gisèle.

1780: While any threat of a rebel invasion by land seemed to have faded as far as Nova Scotia was concerned, the 'patriot' assaults by sea recommenced, vicious and unrelenting. The Bay of Fundy was now a principle target for ships some of which were manned by the former 'Eddy' rebels, burned out of their homes at Chignecto and thirsting for revenge. They seized one vessel within sight of Fort Cumberland, not knowing that its artillery and garrison were being withdrawn; thus no privateers dared to raid our farms and settlements seemingly guarded by that fort. Canso and ships passing through the Strait of Canso were both hit hard, however. The Gulf of St. Lawrence, too, was a favorite hunting ground, where in one privateer raid thirty-eight vessels were captured from a convey heading for Canada. Every south shore Nova Scotia town was visited again several times. In September, 1780, Liverpool took an especially hard hit. On September 13th, two American privateers dispatched nearly 100 men into a nearby cove and then they moved into the town. At around four in the morning they captured the small fort at that place and its garrison of troops from a provincial regiment. But the townsfolk fought back, calling out their militia, capturing a privateer Captain and then negotiating with the roving rebel pirates for a prisoner exchange. They managed to restore the 'status quo' and the privateers sailed off with less than their usual complement of spoils.

1780: The year began with such great promise for British fortunes in the southern colonies; but the year would end with a dark omen. On October 7, 1780, 'loyalist' militia in the Carolinas, learning of a planned rebel attack, attempted to join with General Cornwallis's much larger force, but were cut off and surrounded by the rebels before they could merge. The fighting erupted at a place called, ironically, 'Kings Mountain'. It was the largest 'patriot' versus 'loyalist' clash of the war and it was a resounding rebel victory. Cornwallis was now becoming very concerned that, despite some major British successes, the rebels continued to field an effective fighting force, seemed well-supplied and were inflicting significant casualties on British forces. He sought to crush the main rebel army led by a General Greene and pursued him around the Carolinas. General Cornwallis also turned his attention towards the Colony of Virginia, which had suffered little during the war so far and seemed to be the source of rebel sustenance. Without conferring with his superior in New York, General Clinton, Cornwallis resolved to first defeat Greene and then move into Virginia. He would take the war into that rebel sanctuary and 'bread-basket', possibly merging his forces with Benedict Arnold and his men. Arnold's forces were now operating in Virginia as 'loyalist raiders' with the King's Army. This move, Cornwallis thought, might finally bring him the decisive victory the British had sought since the beginning of the American Rebellion. But, as in every war, "the enemy gets a vote": Washington ordered his generals in the south to start cleansing the Carolinas of British and 'loyalist' forces as Cornwallis moved the bulk of his army to the north and east; And Washington eyed Cornwallis' advance with a view to seizing an opportunity to trap him, much like the rebel commander had tried to do earlier in New Jersey in concert with a French fleet. 1781 might well prove to be the year that both Generals got their wish: A final, decisive battle.

# RECKONING

'PRESS GANGS': THESE armed mobs intent on forcing citizens into the Royal Navy were operating so brazenly that they created somewhat of a scandal in Halifax. On January 6, 1781, a band of sailors, Marines and soldiers seized a large group of men, mostly from Lunenburg, off the streets of Halifax in such an outrageous fashion that the Lieutenant-Governor was called upon to intervene. He issued a Proclamation ordering an end to such impressments without the prior approval and authorization of the civil authorities. This simply forced the practice back into the shadows, however, and no civil approvals were sought. Men continued to disappear off the streets of the capital for no other reason than they were able-bodied.

One reason the Navy was short of sailors was because so many skilled seamen were off making their fortunes as privateers or smugglers. Trade with the rebel colonies was forbidden but still rampant and eventually a Port Warden had to be appointed to monitor and inspect vessels passing George's Island in Halifax Harbour. As for the Nova Scotian privateers, the Admiralty Court in Halifax was kept busy dividing up the spoils of captured rebel 'prizes' which flowed in like a torrent. Fortunes were made by those willing to invest in the war at sea as well. They arranged to build, man and provision new privateer ships in return for a share of the captured cargo. Their warehouses near the Pontack were bulging with goods seized from rebel vessels and this represented only that portion of the 'booty' allowed by the Crown to these enterprising gentlemen. Still, the fact that Nova Scotia had learned how to defend itself and take the war to the rebels did not discourage equally enterprising 'patriots' from continuing to strike the long Nova Scotia coastline from the Gulf of St. Lawrence, past St. John's Island, round Cape Breton, along the southern coast and then up into the Bay of Fundy. In May, a running battle took place in that bay after some 30 rebels in a shallop captured a British schooner laden with goods and bound for St. John River. But militia from along the Bay of Fundy coast took to the sea in a sloop and recaptured the schooner; and later all of the rebels were taken when their prisoners revolted and captured the rebel vessel. These sorts of 'back-and-fourth' battles were typical of the war in Nova Scotia waters at this time.

After tangling indecisively with rebel forces in the Carolina backcountry, General Cornwallis finally began his long march towards Virginia, pursuing the main rebel army at the same time. Fearing that a rebel force under General Morgan was a threat to his left flank, Cornwallis dispatched the cream of his cavalry forces led by Colonel Banastre Tarleton (called "the Butcher Tarleton" by the rebels for allegedly slaughtering surrendering 'patriot' infantry) to deal with Morgan. Tarleton drove his forces hard to catch Morgan – so hard that they were exhausted when the rebels were finally caught. Morgan speculated that Tarleton might act impulsively and prepared his defences in depth near 'Cowpens' in the Carolinas. On January 17, 1781, over 1100 British cavalry and infantry attacked 2000 well prepared rebels: The rebels feigned a withdrawal then turned and enveloped the tired British forces. It was a slaughter. With only light rebel casualties, the British force was annihilated, Tarleton barely escaping with his own life. Undeterred, Cornwallis continued after General Greene's main army. Maybe inspired by Morgan's example, Greene stood and fought at a place called 'Guilford Courthouse' on March 15, 1781. Cornwallis was victorious but suffered as many casualties as the rebels. This he could ill-afford to do. Greene turned south to liberate more of the Carolinas from British control, while Cornwallis continued on towards Virginia. He arrived at Wilmington in early April, 1781, and then headed towards the Chesapeake Bay. Out of contact with General Clinton in New York, Cornwallis's superior became nervous over his General's progress and intentions. When Clinton realized that Cornwallis was finally in Virginia, he urged him to quickly establish a naval 'redoubt' on the James Peninsula, east of Richmond, where he could be resupplied by the Royal Navy. Cornwallis chose as his base of operations the small settlement of 'Yorktown', not far from where English colonists first came to America in the early 1600's to establish a permanent town. And then the General waited. Meanwhile, the rebels systematically drove the British back to the Carolina coastal cities, totally isolating them. It began to look like Great Britain's entire strategy in the south was falling apart.

Officially, Francis Legge held the office of Governor of Nova Scotia since 1773; but 'unofficially' Legge was not even resident in the province for much of the time and the Governor's duties were, in fact, routinely exercised by a series of Lieutenant-Governors: Francklin, Arbuthnot, Hughes-the latter two being the chief naval officers at Halifax. On July 30, 1781, a third navy man arrived in Nova Scotia to take over the reins of power as Lieutenant-Governor: Sir Andrew Hamond. Nine days before he and his family arrived in Halifax, a British convoy tangled with a French fleet off the coast of Cape Breton in a significant action. Two French frigates managed to capture two British escorts from the 18-ship convoy, which nevertheless managed to stay together and escape. Some wondered if the French action was a prelude to a move by the French to re-establish their Louisbourg Fortress on Cape Breton Island, (which I had helped to capture in 1758) but nothing ultimately came of it.

And Hamond no sooner set foot on dry land but he was then forced to deal with the French seizure of ships at the mouth of Halifax Harbour and the aftermath of a bold rebel raid on the former capital of British Nova Scotia (and my home during the years 1751-1752), Annapolis Royal. In late August, in a repeat of the Liverpool raid of the previous September, two rebel schooners with nearly 100 men and 20 guns between them raided Annapolis before dawn. They secured a blockhouse, then captured the principle fort itself (Fort Anne), took all of the men in the town prisoner and plundered every house and shop. They spiked all of the cannons and escaped with a handful of hostages who they planned to trade for rebel prisoners at Halifax. It was a bit disconcerting to think that a place so frequently besieged during the various French Wars, and which had turned away a number of French and Indian armies numbering in the thousands, could now be so easily seized by 100 rebels. The attack simply demonstrated that no coastal town or village in Nova Scotia was really safe from the privateers.

I was back in Halifax in early September to see Jonah once again when I heard of the raid on Annapolis. I had planned to make my trip to the capital of the province in the spring, but we had to make considerable repairs to our 'aboiteau' system of marshland dikes at home due to winter storm damage. This work took much longer than expected and lasted into the late summer. I finally got away and retraced my first journey by land and water to Halifax. I arrived to a joyous greeting from Jonah, now a very professional future lawyer rather than simply the novice law clerk that I saw on my first trip. As I chatted with Jonah in Jackman's law chambers I was surprised to see Anna Chapman walk through the door. She was accompanied by her older sister, Ashley. The two just 'happened' to be visiting friends in Halifax and decided to pay Mister Jackman and Jonah a visit. We chatted with the women and I promised that I would host them all at a dinner that evening. Jonah suggested that we try the fare at the 'Red Lion', a place to eat with which he had become familiar. I secured directions from him and promised to meet them there at around six in the evening.

The 'Red Lion' was very cozy and featured several 'snugs' where private conversations could take place. I soon discovered that not only was Anna Chapman deeply enamored with Jonah, but her older sister seemed to laugh at everything I had to say and had a habit of grabbing my arm when telling a particularly exciting tale. I could see that she was more interested in me than simply as the father of her younger sister's beau; but I was not in a position to reciprocate due to my melancholy temperament. The ghost of Gisèle continued to haunt me, even during my waking hours.

After a lovely dinner, followed by strong American coffee (which was probably seized from a rebel ship) I bid the group farewell and headed back through the streets of Halifax towards my room at the 'Golden Ball'. As I walked along the nearly empty, dimly-lit lanes, I could tell I was being followed. Then I was revisited by a scene from my past: Two large gentlemen walked towards me, the one to my left carrying a 'bag' by his side. I could see that their pace was quickening as they came closer. Suddenly, that man to my left in front of me swung the bag (which I believe was probably filled with rocks or the like) and struck me full in the face. Then another man who approached me from behind struck the top of my right shoulder with a large stick or a peg from a sailing ship. I went down on my knees. I thought perhaps I was confronting a 'press gang' or maybe street robbers who sometimes plagued this town, but then the man to my right laughed and said, "Mister Henry Perkins sends his greetings." I raised my left hand as if it were a plea to stop. The man who laughed asked, "What? Had enough?"

I replied "No, I simply want my opportunity." With that, I pulled my hunting knife from my right boot and thrust it into the man who hit me with the bag, driving it deep into his leg above the knee, all the way to the hilt. He howled in pain and fell over. I then withdrew the knife, swung around and caught the man behind me across the midsection. He staggered and fell. The other man in front of me who had laughed now laughed no more and quickly disappeared running off at great speed down the street. I kicked my two wounded assailants in the face and strolled off.

I spent the next morning recovering from the assault, but finally made my way to Mister Jackman's. Jonah took a short break from his duties and we talked. He asked me how I received the mark on my face and I said that I had tripped and fallen down the darkened stairwell at the 'Golden Ball'. He told me to be more careful now that I was getting older. We chatted on about the war, the state of the province and politics, and he informed me that he had taken a part-time position at the House of Assembly helping to draft documents for a modest fee; but then I asked in a matter-of-fact manner, "Have you seen the likes of our Mister Perkins hereabouts?"

He replied, "No. In fact, after your duel he withdrew his business from Mister Jackman and I have not seen him since."

I then asked, "Do you think you are being watched by his people?"

Jonah replied, "Now that you mention it, there have been some rough looking fellows hanging about outside the office. They seemed to me to be out of place. But I have no idea if they are Perkin's men. Why do you ask?"

I said, "Just ensuring that a man with wounded pride is not thinking of some sort of revenge. Do you know where Perkins hangs about?"

Jonah replied, "No, not routinely, only that I have heard he takes his coffee every Wednesday at noon at the Pontack, then goes down to the warehouses on Privateers Row to inspect the spoils of his investment in the war. He owns several privateer sloops but I doubt he has ever been aboard any of them. The 'Bedford Lady' is his most renowned vessel and she earns him a tidy sum. I think that she has taken some 20 prizes on her own."

The next day was Wednesday. I thought I might just have to pay Mister Perkins a visit.

The following day I stood outside the Pontack about half past noon and saw Mister Perkins emerge from the place. He kissed the hand of a rather beautiful woman who accompanied him and the two parted. As indicated by Jonah, Perkins headed straight towards the nearby warehouses along the waterfront where the goods seized from rebel 'prizes' were stored. I followed him into one warehouse that was largely empty of labourers. I walked parallel to his course behind some large oak casks. I got ahead of him and then moved over to where he was approaching. From behind a cask I grabbed him by his coat and swung him around against one of those oak barrels. Sticking my hunting knife up under his chin I then said, "Give me one good reason I should not shove this knife up through your skull."

He choked and said, "Why would you want to do that? You must be operating under some misapprehension. I have no quarrel with you Hawkins."

I said, "Maybe it is because you had your toughs try to beat me down the night before last in a street not far from here. They were not very successful and came away from that encounter a bit worse for wear. Any particular reason you set them on that course of action?"

He gave a look of acknowledgement and said to me, "Honour. I was so completely dishonoured by our duel and the fact that I was beaten by a common man that I became obsessed with seeking revenge. I told my men to watch Mister Jackman's place and when you finally showed up again to visit with your son, to arrange to put a severe beating to you."

I replied, "Honour would have demanded that you administer the beating yourself, but I am guessing that is not how you do business. In any case, here is what I have to tell you: I am a former ranger. I fought a bloody war against the French and Indians for many years and during that time I learned how to approach and kill a man in a very stealthy fashion. You could put twenty of your ruffians around your house and I would still get in there in the dead of night. The only sense you would have that I was about would be during the few moments between when I cut your throat in your sleep and when you bled out. Now listen carefully. If I ever see or hear tell of you, or anyone associated with you, near to me, any member of my family or any of our friends, ever again, I will come and visit you in the night. Do you understand?"

He choked again, looked down at my knife and said, "Perfectly." I replied, "Alright then. Have a nice afternoon" and disappeared into the depths of the warehouse. We had no more problems with Mister Henry Perkins or his associates after my visit with him. I heard from Jonah, years later, that Perkins was killed by a Mister Finn during one of his infamous duels at Point Pleasant. Serves him right, I thought.

After one more night of entertaining the Chapman ladies, both I and they had to take our leave and return to Chignecto- they by ship, me by canoe. Again, I gave Jonah a few pounds to get him through the hard times, despite the fact that he now had two employments. I then informed him that it may be quite some time before I could get back to Halifax to see him. I thought that Jonah needed some time alone to put his own stamp on his life. He and I walked the Chapman sisters to their schooner in order to see them off. Ashley Chapman made a point of saying that she hoped to come and visit me often at 'Stonehaven Reborn' when I returned home. I stammered a bit and wished her a pleasant voyage. Anna Chapman knelt her head on Jonah's shoulder the entire time while we waited for the boarding and I saw the couple steal a kiss just before she went on the vessel. It was a touching moment.

The schooner the Chapmans sailed aboard was the 'Planter's Pride'. It was only lightly armed and it was bound for first, Minas and then, Chignecto with assorted cargo. While rounding Cape Sable the schooner was hailed by the rebel sloop-of-war 'Rubicon', told to stop and be boarded. The Captain of the 'Pride', a staunch 'loyalist', chose instead to try to outrun the sloop but failed and a fight ensued. Probably out of spite more than anything else, the sloop bombarded the 'Pride' and sent the schooner to the bottom with nearly all onboard. The few survivors were plucked from the ocean by local fishermen who watched the one-sided battle unfold from a distance. The Chapman ladies were not among the survivors. The Chapmans' had lost their two girls. When I returned home and news of the disaster reached us all, I attended their funeral service at a church in La Planche, the town many of its English residents were now referring to as 'Amherst', no doubt in honour of our Commander-in-Chief during the French and Indian War. Now a second war had claimed more innocent lives. It was such a useless waste and a great tragedy. Jonah was devastated as I am quite sure he had future plans to marry Anna.

With British attention focussed on the southern colonies the Royal Navy's attention was drawn away from Nova Scotia. This only emboldened the rebels and the French, both of whom made a new effort to ravage our coast. This new offensive caused the authorities in Halifax to husband their resources and prepare for a major onslaught by the French on the port; but this strategy again left the outlying settlements to their own devices. Some fared well while others were devastated. The whole province fell once again into an economic depression. Barter replaced money transactions. The debt rose as the province sought to fight the marauders, support the garrison at Halifax and care for the flood of 'loyalists' now making their way to Nova Scotia from the Thirteen Colonies. Anti-French hysteria was at its peak and this helped to drive many colonists who once favored the rebels into the arms of the Crown. The rebel privateers and French Navy were great recruiting tools for the British Army, Royal Navy and the 'loyalist' regiments.

On October 2, 1781, Michael Francklin, Indian Superintendent, held his last congress with the Indian Nations on the St. John, almost 50 miles upriver. About half the number of Indians attended from the previous year's council and the only reason presents could be distributed by Francklin was because of an accounting oversight in the Indian's favour. Francklin promised a new priest for the Maliseet to replace Father Bourg (who was departing for the peninsula of Nova Scotia), but little effort was made to appease the tribes otherwise. British power was dominant in the region with sufficient forces now at Halifax, St. John and Penobscot to respond to any emergency given that rebel influence and activities on land had been greatly diminished. Machias was isolated and nearly abandoned. The Indians could see the writing on the wall: In Nova Scotia, at least, Great Britain had won and the rebels had lost. The 'patriots' could still raid, but could not gain any significant advantage. The war here was drawing to a close.

The Indian Nations were now being decimated by disease and want. Their hunting was problematic at best and the fur trade was on the decline. The annual presents they had become accustomed to from first, the French, and later the British, were discontinued. The tribes petitioned for Crown-protected 'reserve' sites at important camping places and several were confirmed by Nova Scotia's Governor and Council, including Aukpaque above Saint Anne's Point on the St. John River; but these tracts were trivial compared to the vast territories over which they once roamed. While the Indian tribes were not confined to their new 'reserves', increasingly they saw their best tribal lands taken up by new settlers. And that problem would only accelerate 100-fold with the end of the American Rebellion.

As I watched the decline of the tribes and saw the wretched men and women who now sold woven wooden baskets for a few shillings at Fort Lawrence Landing, I thought of Gerome. I decided to head northeast and bring Gerome and his family some supplies they may need. I left for the area he frequented the most, the Richibucto River, in December of 1781. The trek was difficult, the snow was heavy and deep and the wind blistering cold. I finally came upon a Mi'kmaq band far up that river hunting for moose and caribou. Their bark wig-wams and lodges were clustered around a central outdoor fire pit. They were very hospitable. This was not

Gerome's family but a young man among them who spoke some English indicated that he knew of Gerome. He was dead, he said. He was killed crossing the ice to a coastal island with a friend on a hunting venture. The pair fell through some thin ice. Gerome's companion had a hatchet and clawed his way out of the freezing water. Gerome had none and perished. Gerome's family left for Miramichi to live with relatives. I was shocked and dismayed. I thanked the young man, gave him some tobacco, made a show of trading my presents for the few furs that they had and headed home. Without Gerome being about I could never have found his family. But the young man may have been mistaken: Maybe it was another 'Gerome' who died and not my friend. If it was a mistake, Gerome would show up in Chignecto in the spring when the fur buyers came there. I hoped that the young Mi'kmaq was wrong. If he was not wrong, then nearly all of the people who had most influenced my life during my first decade in Nova Scotia were departed: Captain Alden, Copage, Gerome, Major Bradford, Captain Bonar, Major Wilmot, Heather Bristol, Mister Mackenzie, Captain Sam, Gisèle-all gone. Only I and Lieutenant Andre' had managed to survive.

Aware that General Cornwallis was in Virginia, General Washington pondered his next move: He could take the large French and rebel army he had amassed near the city of New York and lay siege to that place in concert with a French fleet from the West Indies or he could move against Cornwallis who was jostling with a small rebel army led by the Marquis de Lafayette in Virginia. He chose the latter course of action and started moving south, while deceiving the British at New York into believing that they were his next target. The French fleet in the Caribbean lead by the Comte de Grasse headed for the Chesapeake Bay. With that fleet came additional French troops who would soon join with Washington's converging forces. By the end of August, 1781, Cornwallis was blockaded by the French fleet at Yorktown, the 'naval redoubt' which both he and General Clinton thought would be Cornwallis' sanctuary. Cornwallis and Benedict Arnold never did get to merge their forces. The British under Sir Thomas Graves, a navy man with close connections to both the Newfoundland and Halifax, tried to break the blockade at the Battle of the Chesapeake. For once a French fleet triumphed over a British one and the blockade held. Washington and his French and rebel army then showed up on Cornwallis' doorstep and laid siege to Yorktown in late September. It was a classic siege that any European army would have been proud.

Clinton promised Cornwallis that relief was coming and Cornwallis reduced the size of his defences, abandoning his outer works. The French and rebel artillery moved closer and closer to the British lines through a series of siege trenches. The British, growing short of food, slaughtered their horses. They sent out foraging and raiding parties to try to keep themselves fed and the French and 'patriots' at bay, but to no avail. The large rebel artillery contingent fired day and night, hammering the British guns into submission. Ships were sunk, much of Yorktown was destroyed and desertions increased. British redoubts close in to their lines were overrun by the rebels and French in a series of 'hand-to-hand' assaults. Soon rebel artillery was pounding the British perimeter from three directions. An attempted British 'breakout' was foiled by the weather and more artillery was brought into the French and American siege trenches. The end was coming.

By October 17th Cornwallis knew that his position was hopeless. A drummer and an officer carrying a white handkerchief signalled to the besiegers that talks were in order. Articles of Capitulation were drawn up and signed on October 19, 1781. The British were denied the traditional 'honours of war' for they had denied the same to the rebels who had surrendered at Charles Town. Still, they were promised fair treatment and 8000 troops, over 200 pieces of artillery, thousands of muskets, ships, and wagons were surrendered. The rebels and French lost about 100 men killed and 300 wounded. The British lost 300 killed, almost

600 wounded and the balance captured. And they lost much more. The clash at Yorktown would be the final major land battle of the War of the American Rebellion. A fleet sent by Clinton to relieve Cornwallis arrived five days late and simply turned around and headed back to New York. In Parliament, the British Prime Minister knew that the war was finished, exclaiming, "Oh God! It is all over" when word arrived of the surrender. There were immediate calls by British politicians for negotiations with the rebels. General Washington, meanwhile, moved his army back to the vicinity of the city of New York.

The defeat at Yorktown, larger than the debacle at Saratoga, cast a dark shadow over what remained of British North America, including Nova Scotia. No one knew what would happen next: Would Nova Scotia and Canada be ceded to the rebels? Or turned over to the French in a reversal of the results of the last war? Were our remaining colonies to be joined together in some form of British Union? It would all be in the hands of rebel, French and British negotiators at any peace table. As in 1763, we would simply have to wait for the results. There had been a reckoning. Now the rebels were 'top dogs' in the old Thirteen Colonies-which would soon be 'colonies' no more.

# TRANSITION

WITH THE DEFEAT of General Cornwallis at Yorktown, the British strategy during the War of the American Rebellion was shown to have been wanting. General Clinton was replaced by General Guy Carleton, the hero of the British defence of Québec against the rebels in 1775. He was given a mandate by Great Britain to promote a permanent peace with the Thirteen Colonies. Beyond Canada, Nova Scotia and the Newfoundland, the only major places still in British hands were some frontier posts, the city of New York, Savannah in the Colony of Georgia, Charles Town and the two Floridas (East and West). Drawing his perimeter tighter, Carleton withdrew from Savannah in July, 1782, and from Charles Town in December, 1782. About 500 'loyalists' and some ordnance were sent directly from Charles Town to Halifax and housed there. Remaining 'loyalists' with their slaves, any black men who took up the British promise of freedom if they fought for the Crown, and the various British and 'loyalist' regiments, were evacuated from Charles Town to New York. The rebels then swarmed the southern cities and defeated any remaining armed 'loyalist' holdouts. It soon became clear that Carleton was intent on evacuating New York as well. But where would the British and 'loyalists' go?

The war on land was finally over. The war at sea continued. The rebel privateers tried to accumulate as much 'booty' as possible from Nova Scotia before a peace was declared. And they employed two new tactics: Ransom and sailing together in 'packs', like wolves. In mid-March, 1782, for instance, an American privateer captured a vessel near Lunenburg but later ransomed it; then in June, a small fleet of five or six rebel vessels mounted a more substantial raid, setting 100 men on shore near Lunenburg who then moved towards the town. They spiked the cannons, burned houses, fired on a blockhouse, and then left with their spoils. The town was short of men at the time (who were off trading, fishing or privateering) and, therefore, the militia was largely unable to effectively counter the raiders. But not every encounter went so favourably for the 'patriots': On May 28th, a second major engagement was fought off the Sambro Light at the edge of Halifax Harbour. The Royal Navy brig HMS 'Observer' was returning to port and was approached by a rebel privateer, the 'Jack', which turned and ran when it was discovered that their prey was, in fact, a Royal Navy warship. The 'Observer' chased the 'Jack' for two hours and a terrific fight ensued when it caught her. Sails were shot through, the hulls of the vessels were peppered with holes and the British tried to board the rebel ship from their rigging. Their first attack was repulsed, but by May 29th the 'Jack' was ready to strike her colours. A total of ten men died on both sides and eighteen wounded, but the 'Observer' had her 'prize'. And also in May, a rebel privateer called on Annapolis Royal once more, but was greeted this time by the British warship 'Buckram', was engaged and taken. HMS Atalanta destroyed a privateer schooner of six guns as well near Cape d'Or. But HMS Blonde, which was shipwrecked on an offshore island, had a number of its crew rescued by the men of two rebel privateers who, quite surprisingly, treated the British sailors in a kindly fashion- quite unlike the rebel sloop that sank the schooner carrying the Chapman sisters. A spirit of reconciliation seemed to taking hold.

The fifth Assembly of the province, sitting at Halifax, resolved to allow former Chignecto rebels who had taken the Oath of Allegiance to King George III to join the militia and carry arms once more. Although I had fought against some of those same men I did not consider the move an especially dangerous course of action. Everyone could see that the war was drawing to a close and it was not likely that a few rebel-minded individuals would suddenly cause a stir. The Assembly also took action to repeal some oppressive measures against Catholics in the province, but apparently the Crown disallowed the move as Catholics would have been treated better in Nova Scotia than in Great Britain itself. I did not feel any negative impact. I had received a land grant and had never been subject to open prejudice while practising the Catholic faith. On the Chignecto frontier some things mattered less than in the halls of the provincial House of Assembly.

Lieutenant-Governor Hamond, who had been acting as Governor, resigned when he learned that he would not be made the permanent serving Governor, but rather one John Parr would be elevated to that post. By July, Parr was in place and Hamond had any hurt feelings soothed by a Crown grant of 10,000 acres along the St. John River. Guy Carleton wrote to Parr informing him of an impending deluge of exiles: 600 'loyalists' wished to leave the city of New York and go to Nova Scotia immediately and even more in the spring. Carlton forewarned Parr that he should start thinking of measures for dealing with a sudden influx, including the provision of free land and other supports.

On November 8, 1782, Michael Francklin died. With him died the British policy of care and attention towards the Indian Nations, which he exemplified. In fact, throughout the north and northeast the British were setting about to abandon their alliances with the Indian Nations in favour of better relations with the rebels. While they continued to promise some of the stronger tribes ongoing support in the form of munitions, trade and supplies, the days of joint British-Indian raiding parties, large councils and significant presents were over. In Nova Scotia, that was already the case. While a Mister Cunningham took over as Indian Superintendent, the office had nearly no function. The Indian Nations were abandoned to their fate. And my friend, Gerome, never did reappear when the pelt traders came back to Chignecto in the spring of 1782. What the young Mi'kmaq told me the previous winter must have been accurate. I never did hear from Gerome or his family again.

The peace process with the rebels moved along quickly. Preliminary Articles of Peace between the British and the rebels were in place by the end of November, 1782; Articles with France were in place by late January, 1783. King George ordered a halt to all offensive military operations in America as of December 5, 1782. No doubt choking on his words, the King declared the new American Nation "free and independent". The rebels were no longer rebels, but a free people. Now the great mess brought about by the War of the American Rebellion would have to be cleaned up.

With the New Year, 1783, Jonah wrote to me while on a break from his work, sitting at Sutherland's coffee house in Halifax. In the letter he informed me that he had heard in the halls of the Assembly that in anticipation of the many 'loyalist' exiles coming to Nova Scotia with the peace, large grants such as my own were in danger of being broken up by the Crown in a move to make room for these new settlers and disbanded soldiers. I had been given 2000 acres at the end of the French and Indian War and much of it was now under lease to tenant farmers. To forestall any move against my holdings I offered up most of these plots for sale to the lessees who wished to purchase the lots, and left it to sales on the open market if the lessees could not afford the purchase price. The pounds rolled in but my overall holdings shrank considerably. Agents for the New York 'loyalists' were already swarming all over the province especially in the old Acadian heartlands around Annapolis and Minas, at Chignecto and along the St. John River, looking for places to settle their clients. The river lots along the St. John were especially attractive to the agents, who went up the river as far as a British block house recently constructed at 'Oromocto' to protect the Grimross settlers. There was no effort this time by the Maliseet to discourage either the agents or the settlers when they did arrive. In fact, some of the 'loyalists' eventually established a settlement at Saint Anne's Point on the very doorstep of the headquarters of the St. John's Indians at Aukpaque, without obvious opposition. They called their new settlement 'Frederick's Town', later shortened to 'Fredericton'. Many 'loyalists', especially those from the larger towns and cities, knew nothing of Indians other than tales they had heard as children. The relationship between the Maliseet and the new arrivals would not always be a comfortable one.

Some 60,000 'loyalists' were poised to leave the former Thirteen Colonies and come to Nova Scotia, Canada, Great Britain and the West Indies. Governor Parr started the process of laying out free lots for the prospective immigrants and setting aside sufficient funds to provide them with building materials and farm implements. Of course, many of the 'loyalists' coming out of the city of New York knew next to nothing about farming, and many from Georgia or the Carolinas had their slaves do all of their farming for them. The wilds of Nova Scotia would be a rude awakening for some. The river lots along the St. John were attractive from a 'transportation' point of view, but besides small plots cleared here and there along that waterway by the Acadians some 30 or more years prior, most parcels were a mass of large trees to be cleared away. But the decision to send more than ten thousand 'loyalists' to the river St. John was also a very strategic move: It was likely that the boundary between the new American Nation and British North America would be somewhere close to this important river. Part of Britain's plan was to people that river with a great many disbanded British and 'loyalist' regiments who would then serve as a bulwark against future American aggression and would also serve to keep a check on the Maliseet who once supported the rebels. The disbanded regiments could be expected to settle together and clear the land, working as a group. It would be no more difficult than soldiering-except for the severe winter weather in those parts.

As there was no word yet received concerning a final peace, American privateers continued to strike along the Nova Scotia coast. One such privateer, the 'Resolution', captured the ship 'Betsy' and ransomed her; But these attacks started to drop off in April when news of the preliminary peace arrived at Halifax: No one wanted to be identified as a 'pirate' rather than a 'privateer' once the final peace was declared. And a final peace between the Americans and Great Britain was signed on September 3, 1783. On November 3, 1783, the British finally evacuated their enclave at the city of New York.

In all, almost 33,000 white 'loyalists' were brought to Nova Scotia, with another 2000 going to St. John's Island in the Gulf of St. Lawrence: The principle settlement of 'Charlottetown' on St. John's Island (named for our Queen consort) had been ransacked by Massachusetts privateers at the very start of the war in 1775: Hostages were seized, government documents and artifacts-including the official provincial 'seal'- were taken, shops and homes were robbed and buildings burned. This island had become a separate colony in 1769 (it had formerly been joined with Nova Scotia at the end of the French and Indian war) and later changed its name to Prince Edward Island in 1798 in honour of George III's fourth son. 'Loyalists' settlers were enthusiastically recruited by the Governor of this island province. Halifax's population also grew to three times its size with the 'loyalist' influx. Around 17,000 black slaves were brought out of America along with 8000 freed blacks; but many 'loyalist' slaveholders chose to go to the West Indies rather than settle in the cold Nova Scotia and Canadian climates. And many freed blacks resolved to go to West Africa when they found out that in the new British territories, land grants that they were promised were slow to be surveyed, were awarded in various hard-scrabble places, and many in the white population still looked down upon them-despite their service in 'loyalist' regiments. Slavery was still the law in British North America and slave holders were promised that the law would protect their 'property'. While there had always been a few slaves held by landowners at Chignecto, including our neighbors the Dixons, the practice was not very widespread.

About 14,000 'loyalists' arrived on the St. John River in three successive fleets in 1783, wholly transforming that wilderness community overnight. Only a few hundred settlers had been clustered around the St. John Harbour before their arrival and some New England planters were scattered up the river below Saint Anne's Point. Now the population exploded and, apart from a vastly changed and expanded settlement at the harbour, new towns were springing up all along the river as far as the place that the 'loyalists' now called 'Frederick's Town' established on old Acadian lands. The Frederick's Town 'loyalists' arrived late in the fall, however, and were confronted with a harsh, cold and snowy winter before they were fully prepared to meet the elements. Many families suffered greatly, living in tents with few supplies until spring. Disease and hunger took their toll on these 'loyalists'; but the centerpiece of the new migration was still the settlement of the various disbanded 'loyalist' regiments: The 'King's American Dragoons', the 'Prince of Wales American Regiment', and the like. But over 1000 British regulars also chose to be disbanded in Nova Scotia along with their families, with the largest number coming from the 42nd (Highland) Regiment, the renowned 'Black Watch'. Its members were settled along the 'Nashwaak' River astride the eastern approaches to Frederick's Town. We received a number of 'loyalist' families at Chignecto as well: Pugsleys, Palmers, Knapps, and so on. And with so many new arrivals, the 'loyalist' population living above Chignecto, as far west as Passamaquoddy, some of whom once held high government office in the Thirteen Colonies, chafed under their rule by the merchant class in faraway Halifax. They petitioned the Crown that a new colony should be created, separate from Nova Scotia- a uniquely 'loyalist' province.

At Chignecto, our family ran into a minor problem of its own in December, 1783. Excess ash and hot coals from one of our fireplaces, placed in an iron bucket to be taken to the outdoor garden, set some old rags and papers on fire in our back pantry where it was set down temporarily, without first ensuring the product was properly cooled. It burned that portion of our house down. But quick action by Mark, Peter and Heather prevented a larger disaster and only the pantry was lost. They smothered the flames with water, snow and dirt, pulled down fiery boards and doused the flames, preventing their spread. When I returned from a hunting trip I got to work demolishing the remaining structure. We would rebuild the pantry in the spring. Thank God that none of my family were injured in the emergency. It is doubtful we could have survived another tragic loss.

The Treaty of Peace of September, 1783, radically changed things for the British and Americans, but not so much for the other Powers. Spain acquired East and West Florida from the British; France was confirmed in fishing rights that they exercised off the coast of the Newfoundland and received some small territories in the Caribbean and Africa; the Dutch, who only played a minor role overall, received some small territorial concessions. All of the parties ratified the Treaty by mid- 1784. As for the British and Americans, however, a good deal of statesmanship and some trickery led to their final arrangements. With a view to their ally, Spain, the French took the position that the new United States should be limited to the territories east of the Appalachian Mountains. But seeking to create a new firm and amiable relationship built upon trade, the British and Americans entered into secret talks that led to the United States expanding its borders to the banks of the Mississippi. This was, of course, at the expense of many of the Indian Nations opposed to any American expansion. A northern boundary was also set, but one of the few 'sticking points' was the precise border between Nova Scotia and Maine. No one seemed to know exactly which river was the 'St. Croix' dividing line and where it ran. That determination would await future negotiations.

Castine, located to the west of the St. Croix (wherever it was), had to be abandoned by its British garrison in accordance with the terms of the final peace. The few hundred 'loyalists' clustered around the fort at that place ended up heading for British territory, mostly around the Passamaquoddy Bay, some towing their houses on barges behind their ships. They created the new settlement of 'Saint Andrews' on that bay. As for the larger peace, promises to compensate all of the 'loyalists' for their lost or seized property by their former rebel adversaries were largely ignored, so British promises to evacuate forts in the Ohio Country, around the Great Lakes and on the approaches to Montréal were also largely ignored-at least for the time being. Little was said about the Indian Nations, only some vague words about their right to move across boundaries for purposes of trade. By holding onto their forts in the Old Northwest, the British held out the possibility that an Indian 'buffer state' might still be created in that region, but eventually the tribes, who were greatly misled by both the British and Americans, were finally betrayed. The British withdrew into Canada.

A great transition had taken place. British America had been severed by the War of the American Rebellion. While my family remained in a British-held territory, at times it was a close-run thing. The area north of Chignecto proved to be the most at risk of any in Nova Scotia, imperilled by real and potential rebel invasions and looming revolts by the Indian Nations. While many threats never fully came to pass, Nova Scotia did not escape the war unscathed: There was the effort against Fort Cumberland and the destruction that accompanied that effort in Chignecto; the rebel raids on the St. John; trouble on the Miramichi involving the Mi'kmaq; privateers ravaging our coastline causing great damage and keeping our communities on edge. Now the war was over. While British and American relations would not always be friendly, and in later years would lead to a new, short-lived conflict, we still mostly cherished our roots, coming from a common British Family. It helped us to avoid some future clashes when they might otherwise have been ignited.

In AUGUST, 1784, the new colony of 'New Brunswick' was created, carved out of Nova Scotia's territory north of Chignecto. The Lieutenant-Governor of this new British province was Thomas Carleton, younger brother of Guy Carleton, former Commander-in-Chief at New York and the man who organized the evacuation of the 'loyalists' from that city. No 'governors' position was created for the new province, with Guy Carleton taking over as 'Governor-in-Chief' of all of the remaining British provinces in America; but the real power in New Brunswick lay with the younger Carleton and his Executive Council. The creation of a new provincial government overnight opened up a large number of government positions to be filled that did not exist before. Not surprisingly, Thomas Carleton filled the new offices with many newly arrived 'loyalists'. They were a tight-knit little group: Many of their leaders were Harvard graduates and knew one another in Crown legal, ecclesiastical and government circles in New England and New York both before and during the war- men like Jonathan Odell, new provincial secretary and former intermediary with Benedict Arnold as he schemed to betray the rebels; or Dr. William Paine, a close family friend of John Adams, future American Vice-President and then President; or Ward Chipman, protégé of Jonathan Sewall, Attorney General of Massachusetts. Chipman would later become solicitor general for the province. These men left little room at the top for the New Englanders, Pennsylvanians, Yorkshiremen, and certainly not the Acadians or Indians who came before them. As for me, I and my family still lived in Cumberland County, Nova Scotia, south of the dividing line with New Brunswick which commenced in the west, right around Fort Cumberland and ran to the east, until it reached near the Green Bay. This boundary made little difference to us in terms of our trade or social relations; but with the growth of the new settlement around St. John Harbour, new possibilities emerged: The harbour was ice-free. Businesses were being created overnight, including shipping enterprises. With a large number of 'loyalists' moving to the West Indies, a lucrative trade might be established. They had a need for grain for their slaves; I had grain. If I could find a reliable shipper in the new settlement on the St. John Harbour there was some money to be made.

The new settlement at St. John Harbour, initially called 'Parr Town' after the Governor of Nova Scotia, exploded into a large and prosperous port; so it was a great surprise and shock to the inhabitants of Parr Town when the sleepy little 'loyalist' settlement of Fredericton (formerly Frederick's Town) was selected by the Lieutenant-Governor as his new capital for the province. The move was strategic, however, as Fredericton was well upriver and not as open to potential American raiders, the likes of which we had encountered during the War of the American Rebellion. Still, feelings were hurt and a social, political and economic rivalry was created between the two places. Parr Town elected to change its name to 'Saint John' and in 1785 was incorporated by George III as a city. Disbanded regiments were settled on large blocks of land between Saint John and Fredericton, and up the river somewhat north of the new capital as well. An effort was made to keep the regiments together, officers settled with their men; thus the experienced, ready-made militia conceived by the two Carleton brothers was put into place.

The 'loyalists' aspired to create a very 'gentlemanly' province in New Brunswick made up of fine churches, colleges, stately homes and a genteel farming society; but it largely remained a rough frontier with few roads and an economy built upon fish, small farms, masts for the Royal Navy and trade. Some of the new arrivals spent a few years in the province and then, finding life far too difficult, returned to, of all places, the American Republic. Others left for England. But many saw promise and opportunity in the new wilderness to make it a place resembling the America they knew before the war and had left behind. The hard labour of fueling trade, cutting masts, farming and fishing was not, for the most part, the work of the 'loyalist' elite, however, but fell upon poor English, Scottish and Irish settlers (many of whom were also 'loyalists'), the Acadians and the Indians. And shipbuilding also became an important endeavour in both New Brunswick and Nova Scotia with the abundance of trees. Soon those provinces were producing vessels which, in terms of speed and endurance, rivalled any in the English-speaking world.

The Acadians who had elected to return from exile after the French and Indian War found that they could only secure land grants in remote places, not especially suited to farming. They turned instead to the forests (lumbering) and oceans (fishing) to make a living. They soon pressed the colonial governments to restore their Catholic religious privileges, including religious schools, but there was some resistance. In an effort to regain their voice, the Acadians began to produce their own publications, created their own religious and civil institutions, tried to enter the professions and run for elected office. Slowly, they achieved some success.

It was not the same with the Indian Nations. They were not disposed to farming, which was encouraged by the governments, but instead roamed the countryside in search of fish and game to eat and furs to sell, which sometimes brought them into conflict with the new settlers. Their lifestyle was considered 'idle' by the governments in Fredericton and Halifax and was discouraged. In New Brunswick, a religious society opened a school in the Sussex Vale area designed to teach Indian children how to integrate among the English. It appears to be well on its way to becoming a dismal failure and is always on the verge of closing its doors. The Indians, too, turned to the forests to sustain themselves, but unlike the Acadians found that sustenance chiefly in producing crafts for sale (paddles, baskets, and the like) and hiring out as forest 'guides' for sporting 'loyalist' gentleman and British military officers. Poverty and prejudice began to stalk the tribes. Any large plots of land which they were awarded by the Crown for their sole use and benefit were soon seized by energetic white squatters who felt they could put the land to better use than the hunting and fishing Indians. Crown officials were not energetic in protecting these Indian 'reserves' and some disappeared entirely, while others were greatly reduced. The populations of the tribes declined and it was thought by some that the Indian Peoples of the northeast would disappear altogether in several generations. As they were no longer considered as a military threat to the outlying settlements in each province, the governments began to treat the Mi'kmaq and Maliseet essentially as 'indigent' peoples in need of relief. Somehow the two Indian Nations survived and persevered.

In 1787 I finally resolved to see if I could not come to fair terms with a shipper in Saint John to have my grain sent to the West Indies. When I arrived in the new city, I was directed by some fellows at a local coffee house to a business at the intersection of Charlotte and Broad streets. When I got there I was shown into an office to meet the proprietor, a Mister Arnold. It was, of course, Benedict Arnold, former rebel general, traitor to the 'patriot' side and now 'loyalist' settler. He had come from England to Saint John, where before the final peace he had fled hoping to become an advisor to the Tory government on war matters. But the government fell, and the new Whig administration had little use for Arnold, so he headed for Nova Scotia first, then New Brunswick.

I was told later that he not only owned a fine 2 ½ story home in Saint John but had purchased several other lots around the city, several wharves on the harbour, blocks of land along the river and another house in Fredericton where he carried on some business affairs. And it seems that it was not simply business 'affairs' that he carried on, for he was father to an illegitimate son (named 'John', although he did not use the 'Arnold' last name) with a Saint John woman while his wife was away visiting in Philadelphia. His wife, Peggy actually joined us at the office the day I discussed business with Arnold. She was lovely, flirtatious and spoke of the endless social events she must attend to. She must have felt very confined indeed, however, as she once presided over the social circles in populous Philadelphia. Now she had to try to reconstitute those circles in the rather small 'pond' of Saint John. As for her husband, I found Benedict Arnold to be overbearing and blunt to the point of being insulting.

I discussed with him my plans to ship my grain to the West Indies once I got it to Saint John from Chignecto, and what I thought a fair price would be for the shipping. Arnold laughed and said, "Surely you jest. I am not running a charity here. If I did as you are suggesting Mister Hawkins I would end up penniless in this wilderness!" He then gave me a rather inflated price for the shipping and presented it to me on a 'take it or leave it' basis. I left it and went elsewhere. I went back to the coffee house and after making further inquiries I found a Mister Ryan Hughes prepared to ship my grain to the West Indies and then have it sold there at a fair price. While I never made a great deal of profit on the shipments, I was still better off than if I had gone with what Mister Arnold had offered me.

Benedict Arnold did contribute to the New Brunswick economy somewhat, having a ship built at Maugerville on the St. John River near Grimross. He called the vessel the 'Lord Sheffield' and he entered into the regional and West Indies trade with that ship. Ironically, he did some business with former rebel Colonel John

Allan, now living near Passamaquoddy, just across the American boundary. But Arnold had a habit of not paying his debts on time (some would say, not at all) and used the courts in the province as both a 'sword' and 'shield'. He made many enemies. When Arnold's office and warehouse buildings in Saint John caught fire and burned to the ground, one rival accused Arnold of torching the place himself for the insurance proceeds. Arnold sued him for defamation and won, but was awarded only a pittance by the jury. He later became so unpopular in the town, due to his business dealings, constant litigation and his character, that he was burned in effigy by a mob. By 1791 Benedict Arnold had enough. He sailed for England never to return, having sold most of his homes, lands and other holdings, although he bequeathed some of that property by Will. Provision was made for his illegitimate son in Saint John.

At Chignecto life went on as usual, revolving around the seasons. At age 17 my daughter Heather, our youngest, decided to marry a Mister Aaron Purdy, a livestock seller who resided north of Chignecto at a prosperous little crossroads town near the mouth of the Memerancook River ('Memerancook' now taking on the name 'Memramcook' with the new settlers). I consented to the marriage and she moved away to be there. I liked her husband very much and we visited them often. My son Peter stayed on at home and we ran the farm together, eventually hiring a young Mister Christopher Allan as a farmhand-a relation of John Allan, that infamous local rebel. John Allan had been reunited with his paroled wife and children in 1778 and resided on an island near Passamaquoddy for a time. Most of the other rebel families-including the Eddys'-had long since departed the province for America. My son Mark left to work in Halifax in the building trade and he and Jonah shared accommodations for a time. Eventually, both became financially well-off and married: Mark to a Molly Daniels and Jonah to a local social 'butterfly', Cynthia Sampson. By that time Jonah had become a successful solicitor assisting Mister Jackman with his growing practice in land disputes and business affairs. He moved out of

Halifax to its fringes and bought a small estate in the vicinity of old Fort Sackville on the Bedford Basin. It was a beautiful spot and I and Peter sometimes went to stay there. As for me, I spent more time in the wilderness where I was most comfortable. On occasion, I would walk the winding road leading up to the crumbling Fort Cumberland. Standing there, looking out over the vast marsh and basin spread before me, I would think of the many 'close calls' I endured in and around that place during two wars. I also remembered standing watch at that place towards the end of the French and Indian War, straining my eyes for any hint of Gisèle walking on the snowy horizon. God, how I missed her. And some nights at home in my bed in the middle of winter, when the snow was blowing hard all around our house and the wind was howling, I swear that I could hear Gerome rapping on my front door and Gisèle calling out for me to get up and answer.

I will live out my life at Chignecto, farming our diked marshlands among our friends and neighbors, the first families of this place: the Dixons and the Truemans, the Whites, the Wells, Dobsons, Chapmans, Embrees, Avards, Kiellors and many more. Several of those same families mingled their pain, blood and suffering with ours when the War of the American Rebellion came to our doorstep. War clouds again came close to our shores over Britain's seizure of American sailors at sea during England's struggle with Revolutionary France and then in 1812 with Napoleon, and also due to America's quest to seize all of the Old Northwest, including the Canadas (Upper and Lower). Yet, only American privateers touched Nova Scotia's shores that time around, although enough damage was still offered and inflicted. The War of 1812 between Britain and America lasted until 1814 and there were no land actions in New Brunswick or Nova Scotia, although my son Peter did fight with a regiment sent to defend the Canadas. Those colonies were attacked by Americans hungry for land and revenge, but they ultimately survived as British provinces. Peter returned home safely after the conflict.

It is said that after the Rebellion, the American Republic adopted an 'Eagle' as the symbol of its Nationhood. It is found on many of their national banners. If you have ever watched an Eagle hunt, you would see that this Warrior of the Skies strikes fast and hard at its prey when it is ravenous: I know this first-hand for I was in Nova Scotia during the American Rebellion and watched the Eagle strike. It is a frightful sight. I pray I do not witness it again or need to record any more tragic events.

Bryan Hawkins at 'Stonehaven Reborn' in Chignecto, Nova Scotia, April, 1815.